Bittersweet

Stories of tainted desire

By Amber Hipple

ISBN: 978-1-905091-31-7

Published by Logical-Lust Publications © 2009

Cover photo courtesy of Amber Hipple.
Cover by Helen E. H. Madden, © 2009 Logical-Lust Publications

To Nicholas, thank you for not understanding

Acknowledgements

I'd like to acknowledge the support of my friend Kira Shaffer, the encouragement of my fiancee Ryan Covey, the invaluable resources of the Erotica Readers & Writer's Association and all the wonderful members, Jim and Zetta Brown for taking a chance on my moody smut, Mrs. Karen Bohmfalk for fanning the flame of my passion for words, the members of Hondo'sBar.com for their friendship, my mother for her open mind, and—most of all—Jamie Joy Gatto for publishing my first piece of fiction; for guiding me, supporting me, being my mentor, and for showing me true inner beauty and strength.

Amber

About the author

Amber Hipple is a frazzled twenty-something Texas native who writes about intense emotions when she finds time in between working two jobs, going to the gym, crocheting, a demanding cat named Baloney, reading, playing video games, and a long distance relationship. Her hobbies include collapsing from sheer exhaustion, eating over the sink, and bubble baths. She currently resides in Fort Worth but will soon be moving to Northern Missouri.

Contents

Blood on Snow

He came like a dream immortalized in flesh—wispy tatters of some half-remembered aching made reality in dark strands of hair and golden-brown eyes. His hands were rough and callused, but the rest of him was smooth as warm honey and the dark red-brown color of Texas riverbank clay.

When he spoke there was a chill over my spine and it began a thrumming in my stomach that worked its way through me until my whole body vibrated with the want of him. I felt that I would melt under the intensity of his gaze. I was immobilized, caught in the view of a predator, and the liquid answer poured from my cunt, flowing over inner thighs until I was dripping, writhing on my back and begging.

It was a summer day, hot and humid. The air was so thick I could hardly breathe. Alone at a table outside some nameless coffeehouse, soothing my loneliness with self-pity, I watched the beautiful women walk past and sneered at their fake Barbie looks. There was an untouched glass of red wine on my table. It was dark, sanguine, the color of fragrant woman-blood. I swirled it in the glass, watching the sun reveal previously unseen depths of color. It was a black red like the half-dead roses that had been so carelessly tossed from the florist's shop next door.

I could smell the flowers above the baking bread, coffee, and cigarette smoke. They were a gentle breath of the past spring, a sickly sweet fragrance. It reminded me of Pond's cold cream, of my grandmother and her funerary flowers, and of my mother's roses, scented with honeysuckle, true southern beauty festooning the memories of my childhood. I thought of Sleeping Beauty, hiding away behind the wall of thorny roses.

"Why is it that flowers never smell so sweet as when they are dying?"

I looked up and he was there, standing beside me, looking down at me. He wore ripped jeans, sneakers, and a leather jacket—even in that heat. His hair was a mass of tangles held back with a rubber band. There was an air of deliberate carelessness to his fashion choices. He struck me as a young man who had not grown up.

I smiled, thinking I'd let him pick me up and hoping that I had the strength not to laugh at whatever clumsy attempt he might manage.

I turned towards him and saw the bare flesh beneath his jacket. He wore no shirt and the muscles of his abdomen were clear. A path of coarse hair trailed down, edges of it peeking above his low-slung waistband. I wondered what he'd smell like. Would it be a fresh scent like the river clay that his skin resembled, or perhaps something . . . darker, like the musk of patchouli, a thing of sweat and sex? A flash of his dark nipple caught my eye and my thoughts scattered.

His leather jacket creaked as he leaned towards me and his long, thin nails brushed against my cheek. "So very fair." He spoke as if he were in a reverie. "Your skin is so fair. My hand against your cheek looks like blood on snow. I would like to make you bleed."

I said nothing—just listened to the rhythmic murmur of his words. I was unsure how to respond to his sweetly spoken confession, but his urge to do me violence stirred something within me. A whisper of desire rose to the surface of my melancholy.

"I wonder if it would be half so lovely." His hand clamped down on my wrist. "Come."

His touch surprised me. I feared what this man would do to me and I feared the primal heat throbbing between my thighs. I jerked my hand away, knocking over my wine. The glass shattered and liquid spattered my cheek. Frightened, I gasped and closed my eyes. This strange man was so close to me that I could no longer smell the roses—only him. There was none of the imagined musk—just clean male and leather. His proximity made me uneasy and edgy. I willed him away with my mind, but I felt his hand on my wrist still.

"Come."

I went with him that day and he made love to me on satin sheets the color of sin. They were the deep dark red of my forgotten spilled wine and were cool to the touch. Our breath and sweat warmed them until they were fiery hot. The next time we were together, he poured hot wax on my back in the pattern of a rose. I gasped when the wax stung my flesh. As it cooled and hardened on my skin I wondered if I would bear a new scar. I went to him again for a third time and he bound me with silk, running it between my legs so that, as I struggled away from his cruel teeth, my clit throbbed against it. In the end, I gyrated so much that I brought on my own climax while he watched me with hooded eyes.

Each time we were together, there was something new and worse and crueler. It served only to fuel the slow-burning fire that he had stoked in my brain. He was untamed, untouched—pure and beautiful in his wildness. I was drawn like a moth to a flame. The agony and self-loathing in me slunk on low-belly to his arrogance, his punishment, like a dog to a cruel Master. As if watching a tragic accident with grim satisfaction, I could not turn away from him. Always, I wondered what travesties he had devised for me.

Then one day, he was silent. He was a man of few words, but his lack of even rudimentary speech stung me. Still, I knelt with my hands on his hips as I worked his cock with my lips and tongue, trying to draw the thick salty cum from him. I savored the hidden spice of his nether skin and I needed his essence, wanting to bathe in the pearly drops. Strong, viselike fingers pulled me away and the back of his hand cracked against my numb mouth. Tears formed in my eyes and the taste of blood on my throbbing lips mixed in a strange harmony with the lingering flavors of him.

He lowered his face next to mine as I knelt, ashamed, on the cold tile of his living room. His thumbs wiped away my tears and then he stood, sucking the moisture from them. I closed my eyes to his actions—I knew he relished the sight of my tears. If I had wept tears into a golden cup, he would have taken communion, drinking deeply of my pain.

Eventually, he grew tired of watching me kneel motionless on his floor, and I said nothing as he took my wrist and led me to his bed. Cold metal snapped around my wrists and ankles as he handcuffed me, belly down, to the brass posts.

Spread-eagled, exposed and helpless, I quivered like a jumble of exposed nerves. Fear and desire coiled inside my tense body like a heavy lump. He stroked the broad expanse of my back and each feathery touch made me jump. My breath caught in my throat and the wetness between my thighs increased. As he whispered in my ear of the dark things he would do to me, I watched his cock rise, slowly and steadily.

"I promised to make you bleed. I have razors for you, little bird, little quivering bird. Glorious razors, sharpened to surgical precision."

Panic engulfed over me, but I could not move. Yes, he would make me bleed. Not content to lick the tears from my cheeks, not content to feel the way I ached for him, he wanted to exact my most precious thing—the liquid of my life. I felt the kiss of the cold metal once again, this time on my back. I could smell the metal of the handcuffs and the razors, like old pennies in the air, and a coppery taste like blood filled my mouth.

Then there was the sharpness—the bite of the razor's edge. Fire exploded behind my eyelids as the agony ripped through me. He drew the blade down the length of my back, tracing the curve of my spine in a slow deliberate arc. I knew he would not destroy my beauty and that it was no deeper than a paper cut or any other scratch, but it was all these pains multiplied a hundredfold. Knowing that he was so purposefully cutting me, with such precision— knowing the reality—made it so . . . exquisite. He was savoring my pain, and so was I.

I could feel the texture of his tongue as he lapped the warm blood from my back, stinging me with his saliva. His fingers were inside me, stroking my walls as he cut another line across my skin. He fluttered his fingertips in an inner dance against my intimate flesh, then razor and fingers withdrew.

Again and again he did this thing to me. Lost in a haze of pain, I gave up trying to predict his movements. Each cut seemed to last an eternity. I held my breath, willing it to stop and yet, to never end. Minutes, maybe hours, passed as he brought me closer to the crest of my orgasm before withdrawing each time at that crucial instance. In the end, the blade penetrated one final time and I came. It was a violent thing. I bucked against the handcuffs—my wrists and ankles already rubbed raw. My legs trembled and my walls contracted on emptiness. My whole body became spastic.

He took me then, plunging into me from behind. His hand intertwined in my hair and the other rested on my back. Salty sweat stung my wounds anew as his palm moved smoothly over me, sticky with my own blood as he fucked me. He rammed himself into me and met no resistance. His cock was cooler, but I engulfed him within me and felt like a furnace that would burn him to cinders. I was feverish and delirious.

I could hear him behind me, panting and moaning as he slid in and out. His tempo livened with every thrust, his balls bouncing against my lips in a quickening beat. The force of it had my body shaking. My breasts were mashed against the bed, my pebbled nipples brushing the rough blanket. There were no satin sheets this time and I knew he had done it on purpose, wanting my nipples to chafe.

Bound as I was, I couldn't do anything to aid his movements—I could only pant and moan along with him, drunk with my helplessness. He tugged my head up and back by my long hair. His thrusts were primal, angry, and beneath that I could hear the gritting of his teeth. He pulled out when he came, letting the semen coat my sex with its warmth—more heat added to my already burning skin.

He rubbed the new slickness on my clit with the head of his still half-hard cock as his bloody palms pulled me up and cupped my breasts. There were red handprints on my stomach and covering my pink nipples. Oh, my nipples were so raw and my clit so sensitive that his touches brought fresh pain—white-hot electric pain that shot through me, ending in my toes. I struggled to draw my cunt away from him, away from his questing dick and his bloodied hands, but he was relentless.

I thought that was the end, that surely I would die from it—*le petit mort*—as one more orgasm moved through me as hard as before. I was left gasping, sobbing, and still shuddering in its wake. He moved away from me then, withdrawing his flesh from mine and breaking off contact. He unbound me and let me collapse against the bed. I curled up into a ball, hugging myself and pressing my thighs together to prolong the throbbing aftermath in my clit. In pain and in ecstasy, I could not speak . . . but finally, he did.

Smiling down at me, he spoke softly. "I was right. Like blood on snow."

Kassandra

The phone cord coils heavy in my hand like a great snake or the dark mass of her hair, slick as oiled silk. She is my Kassandra. It's Kassandra with a capital Greek 'K'. She is my daughter of ancient Troy with her dark eyes and darker skin and even darker hair—my prophetess and my hetaera all rolled into one. She has bare arms and eyes like star-strewn heavens. Her name is like a prayer and she is my diva, in the classical sense of the word.

Artemis, Athena, Aphrodite, Hera, Leto, the Muses, Eumenides and the Fates, Isis, Innanna, Ishtar, Astarte, Bast, Helen of Troy, dryad, naiad, nymph, Venus—she is all these and more whose names lie forgotten beneath the sands of time. She is love, tracing her star across the heavens. She is the thread of life from start to finish, the earthly bosom from which I sprang and to which I would return. Life is beauty and beauty begins with her. In her arms I would be happy to die a hundred deaths, filled nigh to bursting with love for her, and wonder, and awe. I am reborn in her smile and in her laughter.

The phone cord coils heavy in my hand like the weight of her dark hair. I wish it would ring. I want it to ring. I want it to be her. I want my imagination to become clairvoyance.

RING

Cue the breathy voice with seduction ripe and rich in her tone and inflection. Moan for me, sweetheart, before speaking in your elegant, oh-so-convoluted obscurities. I only understand half of it and yet I hang on every word she speaks, simply entranced by the way it is said rather than by what is said. I would like to watch her heart-shaped lips, watch her tongue wet her lips, and see the flash of her white teeth as she speaks.

RING

Wrong number.

And again I am waiting for her call, letting the heaviness of the phone cord rest in the palm of my hand. It is heavy like the ripe fruit of her breast or like the pressure of her soft tallow hands resting in mine. I long for the scented, moist, tropical paradise between her legs and salivate over the imagined taste of the skin there—like a bee dipping into her honey pot.

Daydreaming about making love to my Kassandra, I wait for the phone to ring.

I can see her arms flashing in the moonlight of summer evenings and I can already hear her laughter in my ear. She's an angel come to Earth, something ethereal that I can never touch. She is . . . unbelievable—my Kassandra, my wicked blossom, my little sin. I will lay her down amid the tender green grass of summer's first blush and I will worship her breasts with all the eloquence at my disposal.

I will bury my face in the soft skin of her breasts and let my tongue glide slowly, softly, over her skin and nipples. I'll suck like a newborn babe, titillating her. I will let my hand slide down to the darkness between her legs and with gentle fingers probe the secrets of her cunt. I'll let my fingertips dance soft over her clitoris and then stroke firmer as I find the rhythm with which to fuck her.

I want to make her cum, want to trace the curve of her ear with the tip of my tongue and hear her giggle in response—really want the phone to ring now. Sitting here, dreaming of her, salivating over her skin and her scent, I'm working myself into a fervor. My dick is jumping in my pants, throbbing in time to the age-old mystery of lust. I want to hear her voice. I want to confirm our liaison. I want the prospect of our lovemaking to become an agreed-upon meeting.

RING

Wrong number—again.

I sit here and wait still, bouncing the heavy weight of the phone cord in the palm of my hand, imagining that it is her ass I'm cupping. . .

Clear, Cold

She always danced away from me, prancing on the balls of her feet, just out of my reach—taunting me, teasing me with her body language, enticing me to chase her again, though I would never catch her, not if she didn't want me to. She was always just out of reach like a cold distant stat that I could never grasp—a piece of ice that melts in my hot palm or a fish that wiggles free, leaving only tickling memories. That is all I have now—tickling memories.

Her coloring was like the summer sun and the color of jewels, sparkles of light on water. She had hair the color of a new penny—that wonderful shiny copper red. Hers had streaks of gold. Long and curly, it smelled of roses. Her eyes were a shade of blue like winter oceans—leaden and molten, with flecks of silver. From a distance, though, they looked black and unfathomably deep. Wrinkles lined her tired eyes—too tired for her youth. She had glowing,

23

coral-pink skin and thin, expressive lips.

She was not beautiful. No, these things as a whole, they did not make her beautiful. Separate, they were earthshaking. Together . . . they simply *were*.

She was a large woman, a stout woman; thick arms, thick legs. Her whole body spoke the word *blunt*. Sagging breasts with an hourglass figure, she was sensuous, lush and inviting—until you saw her face. Expressionless. It made your mind roil, made you angry and guilty at the same time. It was just a stare though—neither judging nor yielding. That stare was clear, cold, like a shock of water to the face.

I remember making love to her. She never touched me, not truly. She would simply lie there, her eyes closed and head to the side as if sleeping. Her hair framed her face, curling on the bed to make a dazzling halo. I pumped away, holding her shoulders, my face buried in the crook of her neck.

Her skin smelled like vanilla . . . musky, dark and warm, swirling exotic erotic. Grunting and sweating, I felt dirty, guilty, perverted and demented as I slammed against her. I heard the slapping of my skin against hers as I ravaged her—bit her nipples, sucked her flesh—and with a scream I was done.

I wanted a flicker, a glimmer of something, but she gave no response. She just slid out from beneath me, dressed, and went out into the summer weather. A silent sylph, she left me laying there with a full condom on my shriveled dick. Semen dribbled out to pool in my pubic hair.

I loved her . . . somehow, I loved her. The taunting, rabid bitch who never touched, who never spoke except to goad me somehow. Ah . . . but, there was one day. . .

She sat, watching me watch her. "Why do you stay?" Her voice was soft and high-pitched—feminine, until she was angry.

"Because I love you."

"Doesn't it hurt to be here? To be taunted, disregarded. . . ?"

I ignored her question and asked my own. "Well, why do you let me stay?"

She smiled. "Because you are beautiful. But. . ."

I waited.

"Weak," she finished.

I spread my hands in supplication. "Then teach me."

She raised a brow. "Teach you what?"

"Cruelty."

She moved away before I could jump up

and demand a piece of that magic she claimed as her own.

She laughed. "How can I teach you what I am not?"

"You *are* cruel," I began.

She frowned. "No, I am strong. I can't teach that either. It must be taken, not learned."

I spread my hands again. "Then what will I do?"

She shrugged. "Whatever you will."

And I knew the truth—that her words were a delusion. We are all sometimes one thing and sometimes another. We all have a weakness and a strength. These things we learn from example. She was prideful and arrogant. That was her weakness, just as cruelty was her strength.

Something inside me broke at the moment, like a bursting dam. I felt all the anger and frustration, all the disregard and hurtful words pounding in my head like a stadium echo. I looked down at my hands then looked at her. I felt calm, in the tide of my clarion rage—detached, almost. "Bitch," I said softly.

"Bitch? You dare call me that when you are the dog in heat? The rabid, rutting buck who uses my body even when I lay cold."

I stood facing her, her words ringing in my ears. "Ugly, cruel woman." I slapped her hard, a backhand across her bitter, laughing, sneering mouth.

She reeled back and brought her hand to her bleeding lip, her face suddenly very red. Through surprise more than hurt she pushed me and I stumbled back, landing in my chair. We stared. There were no words for a long moment. Then a tear ran down her cheek and she knelt at my feet.

"I may have said awful things, done awful things, but I never hit you. Never." She spoke barely above a whisper.

Reaching out, I wiped the tear from her cheek and licked my finger. It was salty. She looked at me with that calm, cool, level gaze of hers—the look that was not a look. There was an impassivity to her features, a certain slackness. It meant, had always meant, that she was watching, waiting, thinking, and weighing. Not judging but preparing to judge. It always brought out my insecurities, made me uncomfortable and guilty, made me feel a fool and a graceless lump of stupidity. Today it brought anger.

But there was a flaw in her face, a chink in her armor with the flushed cheeks and the tear. Suddenly a woman, vulnerable and lovely, knelt near me. It was almost an apology and for a moment my heart melted, wanting to reach out and comfort the emotions I had just brought to the surface. But it shriveled away, frozen in my breast under her icy gaze. I felt duped, fooled.

I grabbed her hair, intertwining my fingers through those shiny copper curls, and yanked her head to the side. I gloried in the sight of her white neck, where the curve met her shoulder. That tender little spot practically begged for my teeth.

I bit her neck hard, wanting to feel the flesh against my tongue. I felt her squirm, heard her gasp in surprise. Then her arms slipped around me and clung. I pressed her back—back and down beneath my weight as I lowered myself from my chair. I pinned her against the ground and lifted her skirt. She was dry. The head of my cock, freed with one hand from the confines of my pants, nudged her flesh. I pushed myself in, relentlessly. I hurt her, but I didn't care. I fucked her—hard. I ground into her, slammed and bucked. I wanted to hurt her.

She moaned, pressing against me, her legs wrapped around my waist. Ah, I could feel the slickness rising, making my going easier every time I returned myself to the hot depths of her cunt. She cried out, pleasure escaping the thin lines of her lips. She wanted this and I was determined to take in every ounce of her demonstration, her tears on my neck, her hair on my cheek. My back arched. I came in a body-jerking spasm. She still held me as I collapsed against her.

"I love you," she whispered in my ear. Her hands were on my face. "I love you," she said again, desperate.

I rubbed my hand down her hair. "I know."

And now I do. Somehow, in her own way, she loved me. I know, because I found a way to melt that icy gaze, that frost armor.

Fulcrum

Spring has sprung and golden summer will follow right on her heels. Spring is yelling at me with longer days, greener grass, warmer breezes, more bugs, more birds, the smell of sunblock and chlorine, larger thunderstorms, blooms of honeysuckle, roses, and the tang of air conditioner Freon scenting the coolness of my boudoir. I have seen, smelt, tasted, and felt all this, yet I feel the season is slipping past me, away from me. It is always over and gone too fast, quickening each year. I'm thinking these things as I eat a sno-cone, the first of the season.

Over the years it has become my own inane way of welcoming the vernal days. It is always the same flavor, always the same stand. I am becoming, more and more over the years, a creature of habit. There is no other stand that can quite make them this way, which can quite make them this . . . wonderful. There is no other place that has my particular flavor, no other place that can produce a sno-cone of such exquisite caliber I shudder with sensuous, self-indulgent glee. It seems silly perhaps, but it has become a symbol in my life.

This place has become an altar to the warm weather. This is the place where I worship the gods of long days and carefree nights. This is the place where I worship the gods of golden summer and welcome them into the world. Over the years my habit has evolved enough, changed enough, to allow his company, however. He has slipped so easily into this pattern, meshed so well, that I can barely remember a time before he shared in my pseudo-worship. So on this warm spring night, with the sun streaking the western sky with golds and violets, I am standing here on the same black tarmac, eating the same flavor I have eaten since my childhood. Nothing has changed save my husband and myself.

When my lips close around the icy confection there is the same silky texture of ice shaved so fine it becomes like snow. This stuff is silvery, saturated, half-melted silk doused with clear vanilla syrup and tastes faintly of almonds. It's like cream, melting and evaporating on my tongue. I could be ten years old again were it not for the almost orgasmic shiver of delight running down my spine. Spring-times and summer-times past flood through me in a montage of memories—sights and sounds and smells. It all comes rushing forward to mingle in the here and now. My chest fills and swells. I am so moved that I want to weep.

Dirty bare feet on hot cement and long days, the setting sun is our lantern, the acrid smell of marijuana and dry humping in the driveway. Crushed dandelions, magnolia blossoms, and sidewalk chalk. The ice cream man's chime and the odd mechanical shushing of the sprinkler. The icky, grimy, greasy feel of hair dried after a swim in the creek; the taste of menthol cigarettes flooding my mouth. Sticky, sweet, chemical-cherry lip gloss, roast beef, peanut butter and jelly sandwiches, and iced tea. The Big Dipper above my head and the fast food signs looming above the trees, the steady rumble and beat of the high school band's summer rehearsals. The smell of beer and my mother's scent of makeup and Ivory soap.

He snaps me back to reality, displaying the improbable lump of syrup in his hand. He chose banana and we laugh and joke about yellow snow as he licks the aggressively yellow thing. This feels good and right and proper. Our little ritual is completed and I now feel we have ushered in the season. I feel, now more than ever, that the warm days and long cool nights are tangible and not a blur of distraction in my cluttered head.

As we leave, he chatters about the

attractive little cashier, her with pastel colors and shiny brown hair. She is pretty, but too thin for my taste and her manner of speech reminds me too much of a cousin I detest. I am dreaming of my cloud women instead—women who are round and curved and white like clouds, with soft, substantial bodies like cushions and heavy, hanging breasts tipped with red, ruddy nipples. Women with pale-blue veins running beneath their paper-thin perfumed skin—skin that will smell and taste like this cold bit of heaven that I still hold in my hands; a taste that is fleeting— light vanilla-almond sweetness with the same silky texture, as well. Cloud women have bright exotic flashing eyes rimmed with black kohl and thick hair that falls like a veil over their ivory faces.

These women are queens in my mind. Queens and goddesses. They are mature worldly women, mothers and caregivers with angry red stretch marks like highways on their soft bellies and lovely breasts. These are breasts that could feed nations and from them sustenance flows. I wish it to be as if I am looking into a mirror when I make love. I want to see a version of myself between my thighs. I want to see thighs like misty mountains and globular breasts twitching beneath my ministrations.

They are cloud women, snow women, ice princesses of pale rosy beauty dancing in my head. Thoughts of their skin transfix me. Snow queen, sno-cone, snow cum. Yum. I've reached the bottom of my cup, reached the end of my little fantasies for now, my little taste of winter to usher in the spring. He is still speaking of his own women.

Lithesome gangly beauties like half-grown felines dot his language. They would be graceful, gothic-like pale creatures with dark hair and dark eyes. They are unscarred, perpetually angry girls with matte-black lips. Like a force of nature, they are unbiased in their coldness and their destructive ire. Unguided and uneducated, they would be a general force of chaos. They are gamines with filthy mouths, white teeth, and tongues and pussies oh-so-red like blood and love. His women, I think, are as wintry as mine— little lithe spirits of the long, dark, and chill winter nights while mine are the sunlit snow and glowing half-melted icicles.

My devoured sno-cone is my longing, becoming a symbol for my fantasies. His piss-yellow fruity thing has no meaning to him or to me, yet my mind plucks at this thread of winter, weaving it to his visions of gothic splendor. I'm finding the fulcrum of our opposing dreams.

Light and dark, opposite sides of the same coin, our winter women are linked by a chilly, steely unattainable quality that makes them no more than idle thoughts.

When we come home, he makes love to me on the rumpled, unwashed sheets of our bed and his pillow that smells of his sweat and cologne. My hands are cold from licking flavored ice, but they slowly warm, seeking out the hidden pockets of warmth beneath his shirt and between his legs. He inhales sharply when I lower my cold mouth over his half-mast cock. The bitter, salty taste of cum banishes the last of the vanilla-almond sweetness and lets me remember how ugly winter can truly be, how miserable summer heat is, and how nothing ever lasts.

Sperm drips over my chest like a net of seed pearls against my nipples, which are violently red from his teeth. With a rough hand he wipes the droplets away, lowering his mouth to mine. He tastes of bananas. I wonder how well this will mingle on his tongue when he goes lower, dipping his head to my cunt, parting the soft curls there to find my clitoris with teeth and lips.

I never come when he does this. Instead, heat rockets through my body and my walls begin contracting—longing for something that isn't there. After mere moments, I am shuddering and gasping and squirming and begging him to slide into me, which he always happily does. Today he feels like a column of liquid fire inside me. Every part of my body is chilled and never has he felt so warm—like lava.

I slip my hand down to that furnace-hot friction point where our bodies meld and a little further, stroking his balls, making him shiver. My fingers are still cold. I am again dreaming of my cloud women, bringing a breath of winter into my summer, mingling hot and cold to give myself a lukewarm place.

I am reveling in the new spring while wishing the farewell, mourning the loss, of winter today. I am paying homage with a lust that I can trace back to a simple cup of grated ice. As the season deepens I will long for such coolness, but today hot and cold mesh. He and I mesh. Our fantasies mesh. I have found the fulcrum today, though I wonder if it is me he is fucking or his visions of gothic lovelies.

Prayer of this Woman

Crying, falling, dying. A moment, a heartbeat thudding in my ears. Spiraling down and away, the memories rise around me like bubbles. I cannot grasp them as they float away from me, slipping like grains of sand through my fingers. This is my mind.

And what is the reality? The reality comes to me as thoughts, fleeting impressions. A taste, sights, colors, and smells, an orchestra of my senses. It always leaves me reeling.

Every time I beg him to hurt me, I do so with a conviction that lies heavy in my gut. When I turn my face up towards him I feel like I am praying. I am touching the divine spark that lingers in us all. I cannot pray with words when I watch him. Speech leaves me until the only thing left is the mindless gibbering of my want. I pray with lips and tongue and hands and hips; I pray with action; but more than this, I pray with my heart.

He reads me. He always could. My eyes speak to him, I think, as clear as words. Such words I can hear echoing and bouncing through the chapel to him that my mind has become.

"There is a fire burning in me. There is a compulsion. I worship lust, place it on an altar, and call it the most holy of holies until even I am blinded by the truth of it. Kill me softly, sweetly with the touch of your hands. Bring the blood so swiftly to the surface of my skin. Tear me. Make me bleed.

"Make me come.

"Make me breathe, bring me to life. I am a mediocre instrument and yet beneath your touch my body will sing as a symphony. I want to feel, to burn. To crumble to ashes in the haze of this pain and be reborn again. A cycle . . . I never want this to end.

"Mark me. Cut me—strip the skin from me until there is nothing left but the spark of my soul. Make me sob as you fuck me and you answer the horror in my soul. Destroy my beauty. Hate me and love me. Hold me tender even as your fingers are cruel on my skin. Hate and love, pleasure and pain. I know, I see—the truth behind the mind.

"I am yours. Bared and complete. So perfect, the victim, only craving for more. The prey. Come to me. Come to me and show me the ugliness that lives in us all. Show me the darkness that lives in us all. Frighten me and make me tremble. I'll come crawling back for more.

"Oh, sweet pain, you are my muse, the thing that inspires me to my greatest heights.

"Inexhaustible as I beg again. Pale skin scarred and bruised and bleeding and tattered and still I crave. Fill me. Fill this emptiness in me. Stop this numbness.

"Let me hurt. Oh, God . . . let me cry and bleed at your feet, bathe your skin with my tears. Please. . ."

And so I pray.

Reverb

I'm trying to put on my makeup and the house is quiet except for the soft murmur of Sade on the clock radio. He has already been gone an hour and yet remnants of him still linger. He is still tangible to my senses, like the smell of his mouthwash, his cologne, drops of piss on the toilet seat, and the strange adjustment of the showerhead. A thousand little things such as this let me know he has already come and gone, where he's been, and what he's done.

He's here, but not here. I'm not free of his presence and it haunts me throughout the rest of the day. There seems to be a vague impression of his face in the mirror as I blink mascara on my lashes. There, he seems to be laying in the rumpled impression on the bed watching me with narrow sleepy eyes. It's his freckled hand that guides my radio from easy jazz to screaming vocals.

At work, it's the bruise on my calf that

evokes images of his strong white teeth. Scribbling in my notebook, I envision just such a pen held and clicked against his wedding ring. When I eat Chinese for lunch and smell the sweet and sour sauce it reminds me of our first date. It's a song on the musak at work and the calendar with our anniversary circled in red. It's the slow press of my thighs together and the steady throb of my clitoris that makes my mouth water for the silk of his cock. It seems like it is everything and yet I know it is nothing but myself.

I see him in a thousand different places and remember him in a thousand different things. There are echoes of him and lingering traces in everything he's touched. They insinuate themselves into my thoughts. The whole world is suddenly evocative of him today. He becomes a crescendo, a dull roar that drowns out everything but him. A visual cacophony of his face, his lips, his hands, his eyes, bounce and refract endlessly off the vaults of my brain. I feel like I'm drowning in him. I'm losing all sense of myself in thoughts of him, aches of him, want of him. I am breathing him, bleeding him, from my pores. I fear I will become him.

Sitting here at work, at the orange desk I hate, tapping my pen, bouncing my knee, too much coffee and not enough sleep, I'm jittery. I try to banish him, concentrate on my dry skin, aching fingers and icicle nose, but it all takes a back seat when he calls. All morning I've been wrapped up in him, seeing wispy tatters of him like some filmy, smoky ghost everywhere I look and when I hear his voice I feel I might explode.

His name is already on my lips. "Aidan," repeated in my mind, growing fainter each time. It's like stadium reverb inside my head. I wonder why I couldn't hear any crickets.

"Hello, ragamuffin." Mmm, a dark deep timbre that makes me think of chocolate and forested glades; makes me think of some primeval, grunting thing. He fits the description—bearded and brawny and virile. He's my green man, my wild forest spirit, and my primitive predator with fierce raptor eyes.

There's tension and a tug in the very center of my body, the center of my universe right now, my dripping cunt. I want to fly to pieces or melt to goo. My body hasn't quite decided which. "Hello, Aidan."

There comes a pause, a whisper in the background. I can almost hear the smile in his voice. "My nose is itching. Are you thinking about me?"

I try to keep my voice steady, but it comes

out almost as a whimper. "All morning."

His voice drops lowers, a deep resonance I can barely hear. It stirs something in my belly, that fluttery butterfly feeling. There's a tingle that leaves me short of breath. "Good. I've been thinking about you too. Mostly your breasts and that sweet ass."

I hunch over the telephone and swivel around in my chair, casting my eyes around the office, wondering if anyone has noticed how red my cheeks have become. I cup my hand over the receiver speaking as softly as I can. "Not now, Aidan, please. I already feel like I'm going to burst," I plead with him.

"Don't you mean explode, Roxy? Are you going to spontaneously combust like some firecracker, or just sit there and smolder?"

I hear him laughing as he mocks my lust, my desire. My weakness. "You're a cruel man, Aidan." I don't mean to pout, don't mean to sound like such a petulant little girl, and yet that's exactly how I sound.

"Of course I am, Roxy, that's why you love me so much. Deliciously cruel and it makes you so wet thinking about it, doesn't it? Or is it just the thought of my cock in your mouth that does it for you, pretty?"

A part of me is growing irritated at his

smugness, his self-righteous arrogance, and his obvious enjoyment of my discomfort. Sadistic bastard, but of course he was right; that was one of the reasons I loved him so much, that delicious sadism. I still sound petulant to myself, but I try to sound irritated and querulous. "It's all of it, Aidan. Every single damn bit of it from your teeth down to your hairy toes and you know it."

He laughs and I picture him behind his walnut desk with steepled hands and a smile under the dark fringe of his mustache. "Those are such sweet words to my ears, my dear. Here's something else to make you squirm. When I get home tonight I'm going to tie you spread-eagle to the bed. Then I'm going to get out some latex gloves and some KY and I will lube up my fingers. I'm going to massage your cunt with my fingers and my tongue until you come. But the best part? I'm going to record it. I want to watch it later and see every nuance of your orgasm.

"Then, if you've been a good girl, if you've moaned loud enough for me, I'll fuck that sloppy, dripping, juicy cunt of yours and come all over your breasts. Would you like that, darling? Or maybe I should just get out the little vibrator you're so fond of—you know, the blue one—and tease you with it. I could let you come over and

44

over and over, until you're raw. Then you could suck my dick. I haven't decided which one appeals to me yet.

"Rest assured though, darling, I'm going to heap such exquisite torture on you tonight. I have to run now, Roxy. Ta." He spoke all those words in a quick breathy rush, no pause, giving my mouth no time to respond. But other parts of my body do. My nipples and clit are all a-glow and a-tingle now, my face as red as my hair. My vaginal muscles contract on the emptiness between my legs and my longing for him intensifies a thousand-fold, as does the fluttery feeling in my gut. I want to say something, but he's already gone.

Click. Dead air.

I clench my teeth, exasperated. I drop my head into my hands, wanting to cry now. I want to kiss him, to grind myself against his pelvis, his face. I want to strangle him, wipe that smirk off his pretty mouth, and hear him moan for once. I want to drive him to distraction, but more than anything, I want to come. Right here, right now, I want a screaming orgasm. I cross my legs sedately, watching from the corners of my eyes. I hope no one is watching as I move back and forth in my little swivel chair, flexing the muscles of my thighs rhythmically, bouncing my feet tersely, and concentrating on rubbing the seam of my jeans against my clit. I'm too full of him to care much more than that, a cursory glance. His last words, and my impromptu orgasm, reverberated inside me for a long time after.

Let it be Uncomplicated

Hot muggy Texas summer heat pervades the room making the air thick like water. Every molecule tangible and touchable, I imagine. A box fan sits in the window, its noise a comfortable backdrop to a dull afternoon as it sends gracious breezes across my sweaty skin. The bed under me is drenched, my hair damp. The salty moisture traces a tickling, itching path down my stomach to pool in my navel, an oasis for dust mites. The wall against my back is cool.

My eyes are closed and I'm half-dozing in the monotony. A small radio plays muffled rock songs from the other windowsill. The volume is low and I catch snatches of guitar riffs and rough-voiced lyrics. I am dreaming of things, of attractive men and places I would go. It passes time. I run over a list of activities in my head. None appeal and, restless, I shift position. My aching muscles protest the change.

I pull my shirt off, aggressively, almost

47

angrily, and toss it to the floor. I sit there in bra and shorts then look around the room with open eyes. Peach walls—a noxious color, but strangely comforting—pockmarked with two generations of teenage poster-holes marred by smudges, handprints, glitter, crayon, and gaudy makeup from my pre-teen years. The curtains, a converted bed sheet, flutter in the air from the fan. The flowers dance, inviting a person to watch.

There's wooden furniture here and there, battered and bruised from use and scratched from children's mishaps and my own deliberate mutilations. A mattress on the floor serves as the bed. The décor is faintly reminiscent of a woodland scene. This is my room from when I was a girl, decorated with castoffs, makeshift, and salvaged things; spendthrift, eclectic, or perhaps shabby chic. I am only one generation above poor white trash and sometimes I slip down a rung.

I pull my greasy hair into a ponytail. The scratchy sensation around the back of my neck fades. I am grown now, a young woman with a husband and a career. I have made this house my home, a family home for the generations to come. My mother left my room the same.

Eternal; it was a shrine that burned should

I ever need refuge. She closed the door and forgot. I do the same, but at times I come here to think, to be. The smell of stale air always greets me. It has become my sanctuary again—lets me be a simpler creature, lets me remember.

I walk, pace; padding across the dusty hardwood floors. Things stick to my feet. I touch the clothes that hang in the closet—old and worn, out-of-date fabrics and styles. They were my mother's. I inhale deeply and memories come to me unbidden, bubbling up through the years to resurface. They make me want to curl up and hide away. I shut them out. I do not want to remember today.

But I cannot prevent myself from thinking. I was once a fallow field, but now only a salted plain. There is a ravaged Carthage in my guts. What did I come here for? Resolution? Guidance? There are no tears. I want them but they do not come. My eyes remain dry and itchy and there is a painful lump in my throat. We will try again—every night, him loving me and whispering my name.

He will look at me with understanding eyes and I will know. I will know that he dreams of children with crooked teeth and freckled cheeks. That hurts me the most—the way he loves, the way he understands. Those eyes cut like a knife, remind me of my own inadequacies. How can I spread my legs for him knowing that with every thrust into my body he dreams not of me but of a child as yet unborn?

I close the door, light a cigarette, and sit back down on the bed. My ashtray is a lug nut cover found in the street when I was twelve. The edges are rough and tear my cigarette if I am not careful. I rest my chin in my hand and my elbow on my knee. Afternoon shadows and dust motes dance in the air. I let my thoughts wander.

Blood is the essence of womanhood. It is a deceiver, a liar. It is a dark and fragrant deluge, flowing from me and staining my thighs with evidence of my rotten womb. I am no woman, only a poor copy of one—a creature in a woman's guise that tries her best to be real but never can. I am a bleeding Pinocchio. He pretends the blood does not exist, but I hear him mourn in the late hours after visits with my niece. I am a killer. Is that the right word? I am not a life-giver, so then wouldn't I be a killer? The word suits me.

The cigarette is nearly gone and now burns my fingers. Strong, cruel fingers and gnarled hands pocked with scars and roughened with wrinkles. A mother's hands—my mother's hands. My stomach churns and I double over, heat rising to my face. Finally my eyes sting and the tears come fast, swelling my eyes. Mascara makes black streaks down my skin. My mouth turns down into an ugly expression. I sniff miserably. There is snot running from my nose.

The shadows deepen, lengthen. I am empty again, no more tears. Only the disappointment is left. My eyelashes feel crusted and dry. My room no longer holds the same feeling of security, but I cannot find the gumption to leave. I sit there until it is fully dark. The voice on my radio has become cheesy, advertising a local car dealership.

He comes to me then, cradles me in his arms; such strong arms, full of life and vitality. Things I could never claim. His chin rests atop my head. He is warm and the hair on his chest is coarse against my cheek. His cologne fills my senses. He has so much comfort, so much love, and I am dazzled. I think my heart will burst. I think I will cry again, because he is so tender. I will cry because of my gratitude, because of my failures. I will cry because of my bitterness. I will cry because of love.

With gentle hands I push him back onto the old mattress, still damp with my sweat. It smells of sex, old sex, my childhood sex. It feels like age. Tonight I want to make love to him on the mattress that once was privy to all my whispered hopes and dreams. Tonight I want to make love to him with all my hopes held in my heart but with none of them voiced. Tonight I wish to make love to him without knowing there is an ulterior motive, without the ghost of a child that never was lingering between us.

Tonight I want to make love. I want there to be nothing else. I do not want it to be an act of procreation, simply one of love.

I do not want the ghost of a child between us. I do not want the mechanical feel that all our pairings have become. I want there to be honesty again, to feel like there is youth again. I want him to bury himself inside me simply because I am me. My cunt aches for him. My skin aches for him. Every fiber of my body aches for him to touch me, to love *me* and not the potential of my womb. I want things to be uncomplicated again. I want this act, lovemaking, with all its potential for pleasure to be pleasurable again. I do not want it to be pain any longer.

And he lets me lay him down amid the dust bunnies and stale stench of times past. He lets me, with gentle lips, suck his cock until he comes. I taste him, thick and musky and hot, smelling faintly of piss and strangely of myself. I cannot meet his eyes as I let my fingertips trail gentle down his chest, intertwining in his pubic hair until my hand clamps around the base of his cock, as if hanging on for dear life.

He places his hands on my breasts and fondles them almost halfheartedly, but I am not really paying attention. I am already guiding him into me, moving my panties aside and sitting down on him heavily. I am dry and it is not easy; it is hurtful, but it makes no difference to me. I want it now, too impatient to wait for my body to catch up with my mind. The sounds of the radio disappear as he grunts, holding my hips, rocking himself in rhythm with me.

When he comes again I am sweaty beyond belief. It beads on my upper lip, trails down the back of my neck, and when I bend forward to kiss his lips once more a drop falls onto his nose.

He opens his eyes and regards me rather seriously, his hands moving from my hips to cross over his chest. "Are you crying?" His voice seems puzzled.

I shake my head. I don't think I have any tears left in my body. I am drained and spent. The closeness I wanted from him has fled me and suddenly I simply wish to be alone as I had been all day. His nearness is too painful for me to bear. He pulls me down against him, holds my head to his shoulder, and pats me awkwardly.

"Someday. Soon. It will be all right," he murmurs against my hair.

I want to believe him.

Games

It's the same every time, so much so that it has become something of a game. She comes mother-naked, all pale and shining like milky moonlight, into the darkened room. She seems electric and illuminated and neon in the wan light that streams through the shuttered Venetian blinds. I cannot see the water, but I know it drips and rolls down her flesh. It darkens her blonde hair to almost brown and fat drops will fall from the ends to spot the carpet and bed sheets beneath her.

She will smell of aloe and rose that precedes her in a fresh breeze, like a whiff of distilled summer. It will linger after she is gone, on my hands, in my hair, in my clothing, and on the tip of my tongue. The wet silk folds of her sex will be devoid of the slippery "yum" that sometimes coats my tongue, but she will still taste as sweet as she smells.

She lays herself belly-down on the bed

next to me, the expanse of her smooth back bare and the gentle curve of her ass there for me and so tempting. The goose bumps that rise on her skin taunt me and I know she will feel cold to the touch, though her cunt will be like a furnace. So close to me and so exposed it will drive me mad, and the knowing little smile on her plump lips tells me she is aware of this fact. She never makes a move or says a word, she simply lies there while I torment myself with thoughts of her slick heat over my steadily hardening cock. It always seems like hours, but I know it is mere minutes, before I succumb to the addicting and sweetly tempting siren song of her presence.

With my teeth I'll find her shoulder in the darkness and with my tongue I'll trace a serpentine path to the place where hairline turns into neck. My hands will close on her wide wiggling hips while my beard tickles a path down her spine. I will kiss the salty triangle where back becomes ass and rake my teeth across her skin. She will alternate between laughing and moaning and shivering and squirming. She doesn't know if it tickles or arouses, only that it is somehow both.

The moisture between her thighs will drench the bed beneath her and become the proverbial wet spot. The satiny dusty-blonde damp curls are dark and soaked and curling around the slick channel I slip my finger into. One finger there, thumb penetrating the tight rosebud of her ass, and another finger sliding over her clit now. I will have her pinned like some sort of bowling ball. Impaled on my digits, beneath the weight of my torso, she pants while I fuck her slow and sweet with my hand. I will blow hot breath onto the back of her neck, stirring those few baby-fine hairs that have already dried.

Each time, she comes in a violent shudder, rocking back against my hand. A coarse cry will slip past her lips and then she will curl in on herself, throbbing and savoring while I roll away from her to wash my hands. When I return, always, she will be sleeping with deep quiet breaths of relaxation, or sometimes she will be simply drowsing with that smug little smile and she will kiss me once more before falling into sleep.

Once, long ago, we promised one another there would be no games, but as we grow older promises have a strange way of fading from memory. The taboo still overshadows us enough that our amusements are mild and the barbs and claws of love are often sheathed, but before I drift off to sleep with her cradled close to me, my eyes drinking in the perfection of her form, I must admit that this is a game—this thing of feigned innocence and temptation. I do not mind it so much, but her habit of tumbling into dreamland always leaves me feeling dissatisfied with my pulsing penis, and ultimately I feel the irritation and indignation of being duped.

Every time.

Thirst

The sky is blue today—achingly, brilliantly blue. Summer is fully upon us and there is a dry heat in the air, no breeze, and the grass stands parched and brittle. It is parched like the cracked and clumped soil under my feet. I watch the sun overhead with half-closed eyes and I see the lovely reds and yellows dance across my retinas and my inner eyelids in a kaleidoscope of beauty.

The warmth presses down on me like a weight, and I can feel my fair skin burning beneath the blaze. The distant hum of suburban traffic and wail of sirens provides a backdrop to this summer day. The occasional laughter of the neighbor's child drifts across to my ears combining with the raucous call of a bird. If I strain my ears enough, I can even make out the faintest snatches of the ice cream man's melody and I have the sudden urge to wrap my mouth around some ice-cold confection. I feel happy.

He twines his fingers through my hair,

whispers words of love, and traces a fiery path down my exposed back. I realize I am already sunburnt, but I hesitate to move. I am afraid that even thought, even breath, will shatter this precarious moment into a thousand fragments I could not piece together again. Harmony between us is a rare and delicate thing these days and I want to preserve it. I want to cling to it as long as I can. He presses his lips to my forehead, a rough softness I find soothing and I can smell the mint on his breath. When he leaves me today it will still linger in my nostrils and on my tongue.

I drink too much this night and my head spins, yet I feel light and floating. I watch him watching me with a look of disgust plain on his features and an irritation settles itself in my brain.

Our day now ends in a shouting match outdone only by the fireworks that burst overhead. He wearies of my drunken binges and I slur my defense. I do not make a spectacle of myself. I am subdued and quiet. So why does it matter? Why should he care? I wave my arms in frustration and succeed in falling on my ass. I sit there dumbly and watch him leave, perhaps understanding a little better now. There is silence when he goes. Only his eyes speak and they are sad. I do not reply but just sigh and lay my hot skin against the cool cement. My ears are still ringing in the aftermath of the explosions.

I try to count the stars above my head, but they are dim in the glare of city lights. I remember, once upon a time, a lifetime ago, I could see the stars. I could trace the Big Dipper and Orion's Belt. I could point out the constellation of my birth if I looked hard enough, but there remains only the faded remnant above my head, like glitter thrown across dark velvet. It seems the older I get, the fewer stars I can see. I too find myself fading along with these stars. Only a whisper of the girl I once was. Does this happen to everything that ages? Will we all find ourselves pale ghosts of the vibrant things we once were? I am apathetic these days, empty and barren, stirred only by a simple passion. I lust.

Lust is a simple thing—a burning red knot of sensations and emotions that resides in the pit of my stomach, bubbling up at various times to make me feel connected to the world once again. Anything can trigger it—a smell, a color, or a texture. I do not control it nor do I seek it. I let it come when it wills, a tide that overtakes my mind, and I welcome it. I feel young again. I feel wonderful again, like every part of me is electric. I feel like a bundle of exposed nerves, waiting for stimulus. It becomes a yearning, a desire, to know. Lust is a thirst. It makes my skin dry like desert sands that long for the kiss of soothing rain. It is a thirst that cannot be slaked.

And tonight I thirst, ache, to touch the softness of his hair and hear his voice in my ear. I thirst for the feel of his body against mine and the touch of his fingertips running over me in feather-light touches that have always managed to stoke a slow-burning fire centered in my pelvis. It is only when he is gone that I find so much love, so much desire, for him. It never occurs when he is near. Today, I think, was the last time I will see him. There is sadness in me, a faint tinge of sweet melancholy, but not so great. He is only one man and they are all much like another. Each of them has soft words and soft hands in the beginning. Instead, I will miss the exploration of his planes, the memorization of his scars, and the quirk of his eyebrows.

I will miss the feel of his lips and the mole that marred his perfectly smooth forehead. I will long for the calluses on his hands and the snags of his fingernails. I will miss the taste of his skin and the texture of his hair, his smooth forehead and the broad smile that showed delightfully crooked teeth. I will miss his body and all that it encompasses. I will miss these things that we all have in common. But I will not miss *him*, his mind, his words, the things that make him truly unique. I never truly miss these things.

The cement begins to abrade my sensitive skin, reminding me of the fire that burns on my back. I sit up and rest my chin on my knees. I feel feverish, my body holding the heat of the sun. Locusts sing in the nearby trees and there is finally a breeze. It comes cool against my heated skin, my feverish body, laden with the touch and scent of water. For some reason it is sweeter than any summer-night breeze I have ever felt. It is the sweetest thing to ever touch my skin. I brush the dirt from my hands and look up as a young couple strolls down the street. It is a young man and his younger companion. Their feet clip-clop against the asphalt and their voices rise and fall in the low-murmured rhythm of casual conversation. The girl is very lovely and her features remind me of a Greek fresco filled with women in togas that I saw once.

I study her as they pause under a streetlight to share a kiss. Her blond ringlets are the color of warm liquid honey, flowing over her shoulders in a spray of color, highlighted like a halo beneath the wan light of the street lamp. She has a swan-like neck, long and beautifully curved. A pointed chin and wide dark eyes framed by sooty lashes lend her a sultry look. She has full lips, lips that are made for love, lips that are made to be crushed against my own. There are roses in her cheeks and freckles on every inch of her exposed skin. Her full breasts strain against her clothing and her strong legs meet thick hips and end in a small waist. She is earthy, sensual, and ripe. That word dances on my tongue—*ripe*.

My lips itch as I watch her and my hands yearn for those delicious golden curls; I want to bury my face in them and inhale their sun-warmed aroma. I imagine she will smell of loam and of young green things from the earth; perhaps the spice of cinnamon will be the dark undertone or even the smell of a woman's musk. I want to feel the slickness of sweat on her fair skin and trace the valleys of her body with a gentle finger. I would like to breathe against that perfect pink ear, my breath tickling the tiny hairs in her ear, sending shivers down her spine. I wonder what sensations those full lips pressed against my breast would cause, just as I wonder if there have ever been any lips on the back of her knees or a tongue on the curve of her spine. Her voice, I think, would be lilting and deep, as I make a path of feathery fingertip touches along her inner thigh.

Perhaps she will taste like vanilla and almond and the slickness of her cunt will tingle on the tip of my tongue. How loud will she moan when I slip one, two fingers into her warm depths? I could kiss the soft arch of her foot, trace its shape with my tongue, and nibble on her perfect little toes. Would she laugh like a creature insane or beg me for more? I'd like to think she would buck her hips as I lavished attention on the small of her back, bathing her with my tongue. I want to wrap my lips around her pink nipples and burrow like a newborn babe.

The moment passes and the couple continues on their way into the deepening night. My lips curve into a smile and I murmur a soft word audible only to my ears.

"Thirst."

I Promise I Won't Break You

She left me today and I don't know why. It seems I don't know anything anymore. So tell me, God, why did she leave me? I went through hell to be with her. I braved jeers and taunts so I could feel her next to me. I defied our parents to kiss her. Everything we were ever taught screamed out against our relationship.

I couldn't stop. I did it for us. I reached through the white fire of tradition and saved her. So, why does she leave me now? I don't know, nor do I think I care to know. I only know that I cannot pull her from my mind. Memories of her flit through my psyche, teasing and tormenting me. I dream of moments in the garden underneath the mimosa. I can still hear her voice rising to the stars as the beautiful muscles in her thighs flex. "Oh, Leyda, I promise I won't break you."

I remember the feel of her lips on my starved skin and the smell of her dark hair. I remember her soft, lilting laugh. So beautiful. I can still taste her on my lips and smell her on my clothes. Her voice lingers like cobwebs in the corners of our home as I weep tears that should rightfully be blood. Why did she leave? I would have given her the world on a silver platter.

I stand on wobbly legs; I press against the wall for support and travel down the hallway. Tears blind me so I walk by memory alone. As I enter the bedroom a tumult of emotions and sensations assault my roiling mind. Her perfume hits me like a brick, causing me to wrap my arms around my breasts and blink back the fresh tears stinging my eyes. I turn my head in the direction of her voice. No, it is not her voice. She's gone and it is only the wind. My shoulders shake as I stumble past the bed to lean against the dresser.

I raise my head weakly, only to be confronted by my image in the mirror. What looks back is not me. Dark-blue, red-rimmed eyes peer at me from behind twisted and sodden strands of blonder hair. Tear-stained skin hangs pale and loose from my cheeks. This is not me. Once, I had been alive—vibrant and alive. Today I am this. She has reduced me to this. In my fury I smash my fists into the mirror with all the strength I can muster. Small slivers of glass fly out and graze my face. Larger pieces cascade to the floor with a satisfying noise. I cry out and press a hand to the searing pain slicing through my cheek. I slide down the length of the dresser until I am resting on my heels.

Is it the horror of my face that has driven her away? Could she not stand to look at me anymore? Is that it? The ache in my heart increases as I conjure her face. With a thin cry of yearning I open my fists and grasp at the floor, wishing it were her skin, her hair, anything. . .

I realize it isn't just the floor I am holding in my hand. I raise my fist to my eyes to see a shard of shattered mirror. I laugh crazily, realizing my release is in my hands. I can escape from her face, run from her voice, that voice.

I still remember the words she spoke. "Oh, Leyda, I promise I won't break you." I had taken those words to heart even if they were spoken through the haze of lust. Those words echo in my mind . . . *Oh, Leyda, I promise I won't break you.*

But she had. She had broken my mind, body, and soul into a thousand pieces like the piece of the mirror I hold in my hand.

So I lift my release into my line of vision. I watch the light play and dance upon the jagged edge, scattering colors across the walls like diamonds. With staggering breaths, I hold my wrist up. So easy. My skin looks so smooth and thin. Just slash and have it all done with, I tell myself. Escape from the haunting memories. I raise up the shard, prepared to sweep downward and take my petty reward—revenge. I hear a voice. Her voice, and it is real—smooth as silk and soft as the carpet beneath my feet, real.

"Leyda, don't do that."

I drop the glass like it's a hot coal. My body begins trembling violently. I wrap my arms around my legs to hide my shaking. "Why do you care, Petra? You didn't care then, why now?" I turn my face so her profile is blocked from my vision. "Go away"

She doesn't. Instead I hear the swish of her skirts as she comes further into the bedroom. Her perfume permeates my nostrils and causes my chest to constrict. She kneels beside me and touches my shoulder gently. "Oh, Leyda. You've made a mess of the house."

I shift and look at her angrily. "Is that all you can say, Petra? You throw away love and life; then you return only to berate me over the condition of the house? Do you think the house matters to me now? Go away."

She stays. This time she sighs and when

she speaks again her voice is filled with tears. "I'm sorry. Can you ever forgive me?"

I turn away again as her voice rushes through my body like a shock. Wetness floods between my legs almost as soon as the tears rush to the surface again, pain and pleasure mingling in the exhaustion of my mind.

"I'm asking to come back," she says. "I was a fool. I thought . . . I thought it was for the best. I didn't understand. Please."

I turn to her and look at her with something akin to disbelief. Her words reverberate within my soul. "Oh, Leyda, I promise I won't break you," she says.

For a moment I am tempted to say no, but I can deny her nothing. I fall into her arms and she into mine. We cling to one another for dear life, it seems. For hours we make love in the disarray that was our bedroom. For the first time or the thousandth, it is the same and yet so new. Both her lips are as tender as I remembered. Her hands are just as soft, her breath just as sweet. "Oh, rose, my rose. Oh, delicate rose," I think.

Feeling, breathing, tasting, holding. She is everything for which I had longed. Oh, I have won her again, surely, though her touches are hesitant; her hands on my breasts are feathers. But I am voracious. I drink her nectar and suck the sweat from her body as if she were a delicacy, an oyster. I need her. I need the reassurance that we share love and that she won't leave. I have to touch those delicate muscles inside her and feel the breath rushing from her mouth. I take the breath from her as surely as a cat from an old wives' tale takes the breath of life from a baby.

Forbidden, forbidden. This is the forbidden fruit of our youth. This is why she left me. I know, I know. This is why she left. She could not live with this fruit. I can and I show her I can. I try to be strong as we make love, try to pour the resolution I feel into my actions. I wonder if I am too intense, if she will flee from it, but she does not. She stays, and she writhes under my hands. I take no pleasure this time; instead I give. She is mine and I will show it. She begs and breathes for me to touch that inner sanctum. I make her beg again before I descend. Oh, the warmth, the sweetness I lap. I swirl my tongue around the pearl of her desire and probe her secret depths with my finger. She shivers and I laugh within; I rejoice within, "Mine!"

She lies under me, but my mind keeps intruding, bumping away the thoughts of her pink folds, bringing me to thoughts of the shattered mirror. Bringing thoughts of her skirts swishing as she leaves me again. I push them out and push my finger farther, push my tongue harder. Her hands seek my hair. I smell her musk. Her thighs bunch and I feel it coming closer—her release, my triumph. I feel it insinuating itself into my every pore, washing over me, slick and sweet.

Again, her words come. Once more she speaks them to me. "Oh, Leyda, I promise I won't break you." I still do not trust, but I feel I have conquered. Hoarse and fast, she cries, "Oh, Leyda, I promise I won't break you." Her thighs encircle my head. Her back arches and her breath is ragged as she cries again, "I won't break you!"

This time I know she won't, I know she can't.

Sun Block and Chlorine

He smelled of sun block and chlorine. It was a bright, clean, fresh smell like childhood memories and the sweetest summer sun. His skin was burnt Indian red-brown, but the palms of his hands, rough and callused as they were, were pale as my breasts. His skin against mine was like paint on a clean canvas. His hair was a deep golden, dark, almost like honey and it was soft in my hands. His eyes were the color of grass and wrinkled at the corners. They danced and laughed at the world as if he knew something we didn't.

I loved him, I think. Some days I know I did and still do, other days I tell myself it was the fancy of a young woman with no more sense than she had years. But that chapter of my life is done and all I have left are memories of his touch and his voice and his kisses, each sweeter than the last. Kisses like wine leaving me drunk and dizzy. . .

The first time we made love I was at that tender stage of not quite woman, not quite girl. I was nineteen and still gangly with my youth, but my breasts and curves spoke of ripeness to come. He was a beautiful boy that I wanted so badly, with crooked teeth and golden hair. He laid me back against the grass and I smelled the honeysuckle and roses that grew so profusely in my mother's yard. There was a cool breeze, heavy with water from the gulf, and laden with the promise of rain. The grass was vivid green under the street lamp and the smell of ozone and good black earth rose up to my nostrils.

I was sweaty, but had begun to cool, my skin chill to the touch. His hands were warm on my breasts and his tongue was slippery sweet, tasting of coconuts and cigarettes, inside my mouth. He was hard against me, pumping his hips against my clothed pelvis, rubbing the swollen secrets of my nether lips at a fast pace. There was heat and passion and fury in his touch, in the fever of his skin, and the glaze in his eyes. I craved it and wanted it. I wanted to touch it. I wanted it to consume me and I spread my legs for him, clumsy and fumbling in the darkness.

But he found me, found my sweet wetness, and he plunged. I only remember the sudden pain, the agony. I felt like I would be ripped in two. Fire. I cried softly, pounding against those broad shoulders and moaning under his weight. He was the rain cloud covering the thirsty sands of my desert-parched skin or some poetic nonsense I concluded in my mind later. But then, at that instance, there was nothing but the red haze of the pain as he pierced my hymen. Oh, and he moved so slowly as I begged him to stop.

His voice was soft as silk and dark, thick with lust and sweet as syrupy sugar in my ear as he whispered endearments. Now, such things, such descriptions of my attributes, are sure to make me blush, but then there was only the pain. I could think of nothing else until his voice came. It was like velvet against the delicate hairs of my ears, like butter against the screaming hinges of my mind. I concentrated on his voice, letting him thrust into me over and over again until I thought there would be no end.

Gradually the pain ceased, but it had long been forgotten—so moved was I by the gentle blandishments of his words and the beauty within them. I crested the tide of orgasm and rode it once more, eager for what he would give me and for what I could know. *No* became *No, don't stop*, uttered over and over in a litany. Those words became my mantra. I was intensely aware of him inside me, aware of the slipperiness of my own arousal, and the heat that moved between us. I was hypersensitive to the hairs on his chest brushing my palms and the tickle of his tongue along my neck bone. My whole body felt alive. Every nerve ending was screaming for more of the pain that had existed between my pelvis. I wanted to feel.

Never again was there such a bittersweet pain, though our affair, if you could call it that, lasted a few months longer. They were the steamy, slippery fumblings in the stolen moments that could be salvaged, sweet in their own way but never what I was craving again. That darkness he had stirred in me was what I craved—the pain and the smoothness of his voice against my skin. I wanted . . . brutality, I suppose. Punishment, that is what I wanted. I wanted a way to feel cleansed and to feel full at the same time, but I was too naive to know this, to recognize this.

We parted ways soon enough, but I never forgot. I suppose one could say I am bitter. perhaps because he awakened me to such violent pleasures and sexual deviance, or perhaps because he never quenched my urge for such violent pleasures. Nevertheless, I will never forget the spark he ignited in my soul. The flames he fanned in my gut.

I remember that he smelled of sun block and chlorine. . .

Waiting in the Rain

Gray skies, cool breeze, and the smell of ozone in the air; the rain comes steady, pounding a soothing rhythm on my windowpanes punctuated by drips from the leaves outside. It is not humid and because of this, the day is good, but it is beautiful because it is a day when I am free. Years ago, rain began to mean freedom, a time when my beer-soaked, belt-wielding patriarch was quiet. He admired it, watched it, and I found myself in silence.

Strange how things from childhood rule my days—a thought, a smell, a sound, or sometimes just a strange feeling. They have an impact I cannot ignore—a compulsion, a geas, to remember. To see, to hear, to feel. But today, with this rain, I am free.

Surrounded by sounds, I sit on my front porch inhaling, breathing. My feet are wet and the cat huddles miserably under the air conditioner. The television plays forgotten in the living room and I am alone. I do nothing but sit. Right now, there are no thoughts, only a vague feeling of melancholy. I flick my cigarette into the wet yard and watch the curling tendrils of smoke drift skyward.

The cat mews reproachfully and I warn him not to track muddy paws on my clean linoleum before I let him in. I follow. It is warm in here, but clean, and smells of harsh chemicals. I have finished early today. Relaxed and loose, but at a loss for something to do, I wander through the house. I stop in the kitchen. An idea occurs; homemade soup, rented movies, and long leisurely lovemaking. It will be a surprise—an easy night. No worries, no bills, no phone.

The next few hours pass quickly. Humming under my breath, I watch the minutes, the hours, the evening trickle by. Soup sits forgotten, the rain has stopped, and the air conditioner spits out its chilled breath. I have a blanket wrapped around my shoulders. It is late and I am unsure of what to think. I wait.

My lover, my friend. Passion long ago gave way to comfort, to familiarity—a routine of giving and loving—but the feelings remained the same. The roughness of his hands, the little tickle I felt when he spoke my name—these things always remained. Warmth. I glow when I think of him and my heart exults when he cries out during lovemaking. My husband, my world.

I wait. I sleep. Night gives way to a glorious dawn. Golden hues and rosy clouds greet me when I stretch and yawn. He is not in our bed. His car is not in sight. I call his desk. Nothing. I am confused. I sit on the couch, still warm from my body, and rub my temples. A brief conversation with work—I will not be in.

I wait.

Curtains drawn, I am only vaguely aware of time. I try to read. The cat cries for food and I am disinclined to move. He resigns himself to hunger and settles in my lap. I cannot keep my mind on the book. Morning fades to afternoon.

The phone rings and the machine picks up. It is my mother. I only half listen. The cat has abandoned me. I eat a meal of baby carrots and diet soda. I briefly consider calling the police. For some reason I do not. I cannot say why. Evening descends and I hear a cricket chirp his love song from some corner of my home. The cat has found a water bug and dashes mad-wild down the hall.

I do not hear the key in the door, but I am sure there was such a noise. I am standing there as he enters. No words as my arms find their way around his neck and I press my face against his chest. He does not touch me and I pull away, study his face. There is something there and I cannot name it. Tears fill my eyes as I notice his appearance. Clean hair, clean clothes, shaved. It does not look like he has been away. I reach out a trembling hand to touch his cheek. He turns away. I smell perfume that is not mine and detergent I do not use.

He walks past me, pushing me to the side. I stand, pliable, shocked, confused. He goes from room to room collecting things. The cat rubs against his ankles but stops after a sharp kick from him, and I am appalled. I pick up the animal and he glares at me. I watch his eyes. He is angry and I feel I should respond. I slap him.

It lacks conviction. It lacks anger. He ignores me, done, and walks towards the door. Then he pauses, hand on the knob, an afterthought. "Good-bye."

He lingers. Sad, somehow, I think. I set the cat down as he walks out the front door. Before he closes it I see that it is raining again. I cannot bring myself to watch it. I feel action moving through my limbs. This all seems too final. Galvanized, I move to the door and fly through it, wishing I could pull it off its hinges.

"Wait." My voice sounds small, but he hears me, stops, and half turns towards me.

"Please." I move down the steps into the drizzle of rain that has begun, place my hands on his wrists from behind, and press my cheek against his warm broad back. He shifts in my grasp, taking me in his arms for a moment, and I feel that time stands still and that it will all be the same again.

He bends his head to mine, laying his lips against mine. They are chapped, but underneath the rough, broken skin still soft, still his, and one hand creeps beneath my dress and slides into my panties. His finger roughly invades the folds of my cunt, seeking out my clitoris. He is clumsy to the end, fumbling but sending electric jolts of *wow* through my body. Wetness begins flooding me as I wait in almost breathless anticipation for him to slide a finger inside me.

I want him. I do not care about the perfume or his freshly washed hair. I want him. In the middle of the yard, I want him. I want to go down on my knees and prove my love with my lips on his dick and my heart in my eyes. I'll spread my legs for him right here, in the rain. Let it wash away our sins. I want him and my whole body presses into him with that goal; to be his, to be possessed still and not some lonely thing left adrift in the world. I part my lips under his and flick my tongue against his mouth, begging entrance.

I can feel his free hand cupping my breast, and in return, I thrust my hand between us to rub the bulge of his cock. Drawing him to further arousal, I can feel him pulse against my fingers. Is this what he wanted, an exhibitionist? My mind contemplates further mysteries and scenarios to perform for his pleasure and my knees begin shaking as I hold myself upright against his massaging.

He pulls away abruptly and stares down at me for a moment, then pulls his hand from my underwear, as if remembering belatedly that we are outside. He leans in, close to my ear. "I did love you once." There is another pause as he slides a hand over my breast and my hardened nipple. Then he turns, walks towards his car, and leaves me there in the rain, panting, hurting, and bewildered.

With the sound of tires crunching gravel, he is gone. I sit down on the steps, in the rain, and cry. My heart aches, my clit aches, my cunt aches. Every part of me is left wanting and craving and dissatisfied. The rain sounds muffle my own sounds.

I wonder why I waited, then realize that I am still waiting . . . for? What the rain will bring—gray skies and the smell of ozone in the air. Steady pounding rhythm and staccato bursts of dripping leaves. Today I feel free but I know that freedom comes at a price.

Real

Here is a Garden of Eden. There is grass of verdant green embracing pale skin and questing breezes tickle tender hidden places. There is water and lilac, jasmine, and ginger. And there is a blue sky, the purest blue horizon stretching endlessly before my eyes. Clouds and birds and sun…beauty in simplicity and harmony. It moves through me, makes me quiet and thoughtful. Now, today, this moment, I am more connected than I have ever been. Why have I never looked at the sky? My eyes were always elsewhere, on the perfection of a face or the scars that marred otherwise supple hands.

So I simply close my eyes now. I will not look at the sky. I cannot look at hands. These things are more than I. They are something grand, something complex, and I simply . . . am. I want to weep with the majesty of it all—of a lover's remembered form, the azure sky, drone of insects, and lapping water. I will just look within, see what I am, the humbleness of my thoughts.

My eyes closed, I whisper to myself in my mind, not wanting to speak and break this spell. Feel the earth, smell the water, hear the sounds. Experience, blind . . . sensory deprivation and everything else awakens. Everything else becomes more sensitive. Every pore, every follicle, every nerve.

My body is tensed in anticipation of something that won't come, something that would complete this moment and give it all the meaning I seek. I'm anticipating him, only a phantom of my mind.

Oh how I wish—no, how I yearn. Rock me gently and cradle my head between those hands I have imagined so many times. Behind closed eyes, I see sun-jeweled patterns on my inner lids while I trace his skin and etch the memory of his flesh into itching fingertips. I will fall into his warmth and inhale the musk of his skin. I want to taste and learn with body and mouth and heart. I would like us to move together in awkward greed until the pattern beneath all the craving emerges in ecstatic rhythm.

In sunlight sweetness, I'm floating away in my drowsy state—floating away on the molten ambrosia of his lips. It all becomes like molasses covering my limbs and weighing me down until I'm falling, spiraling in the liquid. Perspiration and condensation like breath against wintertime windowpanes. I am drowning but I can still breathe. I am alive and full of his presence.

I'm just another blooming flower of this garden under the gentle touch of his hands. My mind whispers, "There is time. Nothing but time." A moment, an instance and this feeling, this awareness of the now, is flooding my body, pervading my lungs. It is beautiful and I want to weep again. My heart is bursting with the crisp clean purity of it. White light fills me and the urgency is gone. Banished are the hot tears and red haze that always plague me.

This is a healing. Slow, sweet, and deep he moves within me. A nimbus of light surrounds him. He becomes my angel. A blur of a smiling face and the buzz of a distant voice—half remembered, half felt, never known, eluding me. Nebulous, but the lingering tingle of phantom hands is real. The slow drip of wetness on my inner thigh is real. The salty sweet tears on my lips are real. The words that flicker in my mind's eye are real. He is real.

Breasts and ankles and skin and lips. On my knees, no mindless begging. Adoration from my parted lips and yearning eyes. The smooth skin of his cock between my lips, coarse pubic hair against my cheek, and a deeper primal scent, taste. Softness . . . and I let him come into me again.

My legs around his and my face, cheek, nestled against the broadness of his chest. Gyration and undulation. Hips to hips. Smiling and watching his face, his breath . . . and heartbeat in my ears. Pristine clouds, I feel supported. Worshipping him as he thrusts. The most holy of holies and I understand love again.

When he comes, spent and drained, held by my silken walls, it explodes. A flash behind my closed eyes, my orgasm washes through me. Wave after wave, gasping in its wake. White pulsing light. White noise.

Only dreams. Only memories. Only me, alone in this garden staring down at the mounds of my breasts and thighs. Hand disappearing into that slick crevice. But the light is still so real in my dazzled eyes. The slickness of my sex, the tingle of lips and fingertips. I am alive . . . happy, smiling. Somehow, he is real.

Yellow

Sunlight is yellow. Autumn leaves are yellow and sometimes so is gold. All these things are beautiful, but Rebekah is the most precious. She has hair like wheat, her eyes are like burnished gold, and her skin is tawny. I paint her monochromatically, only hinting at all the shades that color her. She becomes simply yellow, like the smiling suns and cheery fires. It seems a bright happy color, a children's color, and so full of innocence and light.

Here is one where she is arrayed like a child, gussied up like some plaything. She is a Victorian doll that stood on her bookshelf, with her ruffles and butter-cream lace. Flowing ribbons are tied under her chin in a large bow, securing the bonnet. Her silk stockings and leather shoes are clearly visible as one small hand lifts her skirts. There, you can see each detail, each golden curl of her sex and the illusion of lingering moisture. When I see this, when I paint this, there is an intimacy I never felt, even when I held her.

There are other portraits in this series. This is Rebekah as a ballerina stretching at the bar, the light just catching the curve of her ass beneath the stiff skirt. Rebekah as a daisy with her yellow skirts, the petals and her ass the center. In this one she is Lady Godiva, bare-breasted and asleep on the horse's back with hair tumbling into her eyes.

My masterpiece, though, is this one— Rebekah as the morning star. She's floating bright in the middle of a sunrise sky with her arms stretched above her head and her hair fanning behind her like a halo. An exultant expression graces her face, a smile on her lips in this transformation from woman to light. Her body and face are suffused with a glow and eldritch sparkles. She is long and lean and smooth with Art Deco lines.

Looking at this painting, I can see the swirls and scatters of yellow that become her face and skin. In my mind this is how I have always seen her, as a beautiful, ethereal woman cloaked in all the shades of yellow starlight. With these pristine lines and perfect Euclidean curves, I liken her to the pinnacle of womanhood.

When I touch her I see her as I will paint

her. In the thick grass of the park she became my daisy. Floating in the pool, I can only see her breasts and face and belly. For this scene she will be the fallen sky-lord's daughter floating in drops of liquid fire. When she laughs and dances in a circle next to the campfire with the embers moving around her ankles and calves, I will give her life in a swirl of hair and with fireflies rising up to the backdrop of the lantern moon.

I can see so clearly the light that blazes in her soul. It's pure and flickering like strong candlelight. I want to touch it when I make love to her. When the tip of my cock presses into her, I dream myself plunging into that pool of light and stirring its depths. I want to taste this essence when my tongue invades her mouth. I'd lap it up like cinnamon-fire from the folds of her sex. I want it, but it's a fleeting ephemeral thing that spreads away when the waves of her orgasms finally subside. I must capture it with palette and brush—try to recall the exact color. I want the world to see her as I do.

It is, therefore, truly a shame that mankind cannot reproduce the perfect shade of yellow for these painting of her that cluster in the galleries of my mind.

White Musk

It is close to Christmas and though there is a chill outside, inside the store it is hot and stuffy. I am standing in the middle of the aisle, an exhausted, frazzled, stressed, overweight woman. I'm superwoman with a fulltime job and fulltime housework—and all the worries of both resting squarely on my already aching back. My red hair is all fly-aways and my legs are planted far apart. Between all the commercials, *gimmes*, and toils, I find it hard to truly warm to the Christmas season. I agonize so much over just the right gift for the right person. I want so much for everything to be perfect that Christmas becomes nothing but another test for me—another measure of my own inadequacies. I long for simpler times when cardboard and macaroni were the thing. My thoughts have been scattered and my eyes are lost, confused. Something . . . something, has dispelled my aura of industriousness and sent me reeling.

I hate Christmas shopping, but I enjoy giving the gifts. I like finding the one that's just perfect, beautiful, and wonderful—something that jumps out at me and screams the name of the person I am shopping for. There is something almost magical in the squeal and peal of utter delight and the shining eyes. What I hate is the Supercenter where my budget forces me to shop every year.

Crowded and hot, there are people everywhere, jostling, elbowing, and bustling. Most do not even speak enough English to offer a *pardon me*. There is a distinct smell of cat urine wafting from the large woman in the muumuu who pushes her cart past me, and the crying child that trails behind her, fisting his eyes, does not help my headache. Nothing is ever on the shelves where it should be so I must hunt for it. Today I am hunting for a scarf.

I find it on a rack marked *Earmuffs* but there are no earmuffs there. I can only imagine a pair of lonely earmuffs occupying a shelf on the other side of the store marked *Tomato Soup*. There is only one scarf—an itchy wool concoction in a very tacky mustard color and decorated with fuchsia flowers. I am forced to abandon the scarf. Aunt Millie might find the colors quite her style, but she is, unfortunately, allergic to wool.

So I continue to wander the store, prowling and hunting for Aunt Millie's present. Until now.

Something has grabbed my attention and I can't say . . . ah, wait. There it is. My eyes clear as comprehension creeps up on me. My nostrils flare and the smell, a lovely thick aroma, fills me. I close my eyes then, oblivious to all the people milling about. I pay no heed to the way they whisper behind their hands and cut their eyes at the fat crazy redhead that takes up the whole aisle. I have stumbled onto the perfume section.

Heady, warm, and so very sweet, it's white musk. Her hair, her clothes, and the pillows of her breasts had smelled of it. I would have sworn it bled from her pores. Intoxicating, dizzying, insinuating, it conjures up her face to me. Oh, those blue-green eyes . . . large and luminous, ringed in black. Flashing, electric eyes. She had a pug nose that only enhanced the fragile and childlike beauty of her face. I can hear her laugh, breathy and close to my ear, and feel the weighted silk mass of her hair sliding through my hands. All smelling of one thing.

She had been beautiful; soft and so white with her pale limbs. Full-bodied and thick, she was substantial and real. Skin that summoned the perfection of lace, but eyes that summoned heat. My statuesque creature. I wished then and I wish now that there had been enough talent in my hands to sculpt her, to paint her, as I had seen her. I called her exotic. *My Saba.* Say it slow, let it drop from the lips like an exhale, a murmured prayer. *My Saba.*

She had been open, honest, sincere, friendly, and brash. She had been everything I never dared to be. I loved her for that. A glamorous, stomping, forceful creature whose passage was marked. Ah . . . but she seemed to shrink, become some delicate blossom, all pale skin and hot breath in my bed. She had wide brown nipples and heavy white mounds for thighs. She tasted good to me—the valleys of her skin like cinnamon. The folds between her legs were slick velvet. The hair there, coarse and curly, had smelled of white musk.

I gave her a bottle of it for Christmas, knowing how fond she was of it. Squeal, peal, tearful eyes, and she flung herself at me, her sweet, full, generous lips on mine, her heavy breasts pressed against my chest. Her tongue was butterscotch and cigarettes. Her skin flushed with delight, a kitten in my arms.

Laughing, I made her beg for me. I made her beg to come. There was cold, wet Texas air outside the window, but there was warmth in her body, in her voice. Sheets tangled around her legs, white as fresh snow that we had never seen. Her hair hung in her face and her lips parted as she panted, swollen from my kisses. That image lingers in my mind . . . naked and tempting, lush and inviting, exquisite little fey. For days after, I could taste her and smell white musk in my home.

I can still recall the tears I shed when she left. Through no one's fault, it was simply eddies and tides of life that took her from me. I wanted to hit my knees and grasp that pale hand and beg her to stay. I wanted to promise her the world. Lay frankincense and myrrh at her feet like she was the ancient goddess queen she had become to me. My magic sparkle fey woman of such cloying scents. She wept too, against my hair, murmuring to me.

In the hallway, we said goodbye, uncaring if our parents or siblings watched. Hands roaming over one another, we promised with young fervor and desire to write, to talk, to laugh again. They were sweet words, but we were young and fickle and love's heat never lasts when love departs. But then, at that moment, there was nothing but her. Clinging, we tried to capture that one lingering taste of saccharine moment before she left for the airport.

For months after, I could not banish the

image of her alabaster skin and electric eyes, and it seemed no matter where I went I could smell white musk. It would drift past me, heady and thick, and tears would sting my eyes and something in my chest would constrict painfully until I could not breathe. I thought of her in Kansas, wasted on the flat plains when a woman in the Texas pine forests craved her so badly as her winter sprite.

But winter passed, giving way to summer and fruity floral scents that reminded me only of watermelon and sunlight. By next winter, she was but a fond remembrance, a sometime fancy in the back of my mind. I was young and life, the world, moved on. It's only now, contemplative, caught up in my own head, moving through my own world, and longing so much to be that age again even as I try to force some holiday cheer, that it comes back to me so vividly. It's only now that I regret it so vividly.

It's cold outside again and I can smell it, in the air, here in the store, but so many times in the past it was only in my mind. It conjures up her face, her laugh, everything I loved so much about her. I am losing myself in these memories. I wish . . . I wish I had savored the taste of her sweat and the taste of the juices that coated her thighs. I wish I could still recall the exact feeling of her vaginal walls clenching my fingers when she came. I wish her eyes were not a smudge of kohl in my head as I picture her speaking. I wish . . . that I had held tighter to her, that she were captured, her image, in a snow globe, for me to watch in the dim hours of the morning when I feel the most alone.

The moment passes and I am again a chubby woman standing in the middle of a busy store. People are giving me dirty looks still, but I ignore them, so wrapped up am I in such a sweet remembrance. I grab a bottle of the perfume. I hardly wear cosmetics of any sort—I can hardly afford them—but I cannot pass this by. I will buy it for myself, a Christmas present for myself. I will wear it, layering it on thick, and wrap myself in this familiar smell. A warm blanket if her scent, a reminder of winter's love. I will wear it and remember.

All the World is a Stage

I am her, living in her skin, for one moment. The lights are hot, glaring in my eyes until I can see nothing but the flash of my own limbs. Sweat pours down my face and bunches my tights uncomfortably against my crotch. No one can see this. No one can see the things that might ruin the illusion. No one but me knows the ache and burn in my muscles as I become the delicate dancing rose. On this stage, I am no longer human, but a puppet, dancing for the whims of an audience I can never see under the glare of the lights.

I know this to be a truth as I watch her. She's an enchanted flower, whirling to the instrumental accompaniment, covering our eyes with a veil of ignorance. We cannot see her for what she truly is, so well does she weave her spell. She is no longer a *she*, but a thing. It's easy for some to forget, to lose themselves in the fantasy the dancers create. I cannot.

It is the very humanity of her that draws me. I know that beneath her façade she is real, made of flesh and bone and blood just like me. It is her humanity that I see when she dances. There is fluidity and grace in her well-toned body and I know it takes years of work to achieve those results. There is also an ethereal calm to her, a serenity I have never seen duplicated by anything inanimate. Also, if one looks closely, you can see her chest heave with heavy breaths after each difficult spin and the baby-fine curls sticking to her sweaty neck when she bows. And there, when she smiles, her teeth are ever so slightly crooked. She is flawed and therein lies her true beauty.

What is lovelier than knowing she is not some unattainable fantasy, but a truth I can hold in my arms? The perfection that clutters our dreams is made of nothing more than dreams. The sweetness is having her here, with her crooked teeth and scarred ankle, in my arms as a tangible thing and not the cobwebs of midnight fantasy. Yet she is an actor. It is her calling, her training, to make herself a distant dream. This is how she wishes others to view her, as implacable perfection. So when the web of fantasy is torn, when I view her with my eyes rather than with wishful thinking, I feel like I am betraying her. It feels as if I am committing a sin against her.

When I watch her stretch each evening I am witnessing a forbidden rite. I watch the layers of her clothing and makeup build up, crafting the image she chooses each night, and after I will watch those layers be stripped away. I witness the making of a dream and it seems sacrilege. With carefully placed feet, timed leaps, and complexly crafted costumes, she becomes their flower, water lily, fairy, whatever, but I have seen the becoming and know her to be just a woman.

I have seen her stripped of illusion, but she loses none of her mystery. I see her as she is, but I wonder if she is simply acting again. Is she moving herself through life, improvising new dance steps as she goes, counting out the time in her head to music only she can hear? Perhaps that is why she always seems distracted, as if her eyes are elsewhere. Even so, I am privileged, because she gives me at least a fraction more reality than she gives others. It isn't disappointing, this reality.

What is more mysterious, more deserving of worship, than a woman in the full flower of her youth? Is there not just as much merit in the grace she applies to cooking a well-balanced meal as in the effort she expends stumbling through a new dance? Watch how she moves in an unguarded moment and one will see that same poetry, the same unconscious moves. It is in her blood.

So I watch her tonight and for one moment I am her. She is all too real to herself, all too conscious of her flaws and imperfections and shortcomings. She pushes herself, strides forward, giving and giving and giving to the audience until she feels she will collapse or burst—all in an effort to achieve the imagined perfection society imposes on us. She makes loves to them with her eyes and indicates her yearning with poised arms, rebuffs them with her straight back and curved neck, and teases them with a well-turned calf.

She is a whore, pimping herself on the stage. She is the dream weaver, the miracle maker—a merchant, hawking the wares of our fantasies. When she dances, she does not realize I still see the reality. When she dances, she is no longer mine, but theirs. The knowing makes my heart ache, but I love her all the more, knowing how much it means to her and knowing, perhaps savoring, the fact that I can see through it. I can see her heart.

I find myself imagining the moments when she is mine. How many kisses have I stolen in darkened hallways before and after shows?

Then there are the quick gropes and dry humping that leaves both of us red-faced and flustered like teenagers. While she's dancing and acting I am sitting here dying. I press my thighs close together, cross my legs, and adjust my hips in my seat, positioning the seam of my pants just so over my sex. Tapping my foot and dancing my legs in an imitation of nervous jitters, I rub my clit in a well-honed rhythm.

I see her up there, her body above me with her glittery tattered skirt flying around her legs. Her unbound hair cascades down her back in a tangled mass of blonde lace with green ivy. The palms of my hands itch to be full of those strands and my nostrils flare, imagining the smell of her vanilla skin. I clench my jaw, cutting back the flow of saliva, as I think about the taste of her juices—the acidic tang of her pussy, musky with sweat. I am full of her and heavy with my own slick desire. I press my thighs closer, tighter. My foot is now bouncing in a crazy, jerky movement that has no relevance to what is happening on the stage or to any of the music that is playing.

Beautiful.

I come with a loud gasp, my orgasm rocketing through me and tingling its way down to my toes. Almost in sympathetic climax it seems, she falls to her knees and the audience rushes to its feet, clapping and cheering her. I watch the dancers come out and bow, the curve of her neck, and the way she clenches the hands of the dancers next to her. I am not sated. I can feel desire rising in me once more. I remain in my seat as everyone else files out, snatches of *amazing*, *poetic*, and *breathtaking* coming to my ears. I am still sitting here, brooding, smoldering, and waiting.

The lights go down and there is the heavy thud of machines as they work backstage. I rise to my feet, smooth imaginary wrinkles from pants, and walk down the aisle towards the stage and her dressing room. I feel like a bride going to the bedchamber on her wedding night. She will be there waiting for me—moist with perspiration, exhausted, and aching, but happy and ready to receive me with open arms.

I will finish breaking the illusion. I will strip the clothes from her, peel the layers away, and reveal the center of her humanity. I will sculpt and mold her with feathery touches into my own fantasy, the illusion of reality. Tonight, I will be no better than the audience. Tonight, I am greedy.

I don't knock. What's the point? I can see none, but I see enormous potential in surprising her, catching her off guard with a momentary look of surprise or indignation on her face. She is standing with her back to the door, already half-undressed, in nothing but her skirt. I can hear the *shushing* sound of her hair moving against the skin of her bare back and she slowly turns to face me. She is a woodland sprite I've captured in a revealing moment with her bare breasts pale like milk, blue veins running like rivers beneath it, and the pink tips of her nipples inviting my touch. She smiles and beckons me forward silently.

I move across the small room, the tap of my heels audible on the cheap, scuffed linoleum. She murmurs something about my suit; the dark chocolate-brown I know compliments my red hair just so. I don't respond. I feel no need to demur with a *thank you* or mutter some pleasantry about dressing myself with her in mind. Instead I enfold her in my arms, sliding them around her slick skin though it's cool to the touch. So petite. I smile down at her. I often forget how small she is. She seems a giant on the stage.

I lower my face to her and press my lips against hers, seeking entrance with the tip of my tongue. She shifts under me, sliding closer, and she gives a muffled laugh as she parts her mouth to my questing tongue. She tastes like cola and peanut butter, but feels like heaven as our tongues intertwine, dancing together in a way that does little to quench the fire already pulsing in my pelvis, centered in my clit, but it is an excellent prelude.

I move my hand from around her back, stroking my fingers up her ribs, dancing them over the bones until I find the curve of her breast and part from her enough to allow my hand access. I cup her breast, tracing my thumb over her nipple till it's eager and perky.

At this point she pulls away and looks at me with a confused expression, flustered and hot and bothered. "What's gotten in to you?"

I smile, continuing to stroke her nipple. "Hopefully you."

She laughs, thinking I'm joking, a little witty wordplay, but I'm dead serious. I bump my hips into hers, nudging her back towards her dressing table, and her face carries a look that is faintly irritated. "Here?"

I take a step forward, holding her and urging her a step back, a little smile still plastered on my face. "Why not?"

Another two steps and her ass is right against the tabletop. She sits down heavily, scattering tubes of makeup and cold cream. "I can think of dozens of reasons."

I laugh softly and lower my face, so I can tease the tip of her nipple with my tongue before speaking again. "Give me one good one." A tube of lipstick rolls off the counter and clacks harshly against the floor. I see her eyes flicker towards it and her body move slightly, as if to retrieve it. I shake my head. "No, let me."

I pull away from her and squat down, one hand reaching out to grab the lipstick, but I never make contact. While her attention is still riveted on the lost cosmetic, I slip my other hand up, straight to her sex. Vested of her tights, she is bare beneath, all hot skin and sweaty pussy. I lay my hand against the crinkle of soft hair there and look up at her. She's looking at me now, but then her eyes flicker to the door. I shrug and stand up, extricating myself from my position.

"Lock the door." She hasn't moved and I feel a giddiness rising in me, so I cross the small room for the second and third time this evening as I lock the door and then come back to her. She's still pressed up against the counter where I left her. I stoop, pick up the lipstick, lay it on the counter near her hip, and then let myself rest on my knees. "Please," she says so sweetly.

I move my hands up her legs, lifting the wispy pieces of her skirt as I go, flinging it up and around her waists, exposing her pelvis to my eyes; the deep V of her sex, covered with a fine pelt of dark-blonde curls. I let my fingers dance through her curls for a moment and then part her legs. I can already smell the sweet heady musk of her. I am absorbed in the spectacle before me as I let one of my fingers slowly travel the length of her lips and back again. I part her folds gently, running my finger once more from the entrance of her sex to the tip of her clitoris, and she thrusts her hips towards me as I make contact with that nub.

I dip my head down, using forefinger and thumb to part her lips fully, displaying the desired fruit to my questing tongue. She tastes of salt and soap and feels of warm, slippery heat. I can feel the tingle of her juices on my tongue already as I flick it quickly, back and forth over her clit. She shivers in response, reaching down with her small hands to grasp my head and press my face closer. I burrow like a newborn rooting for sustenance. I inhale her scent and draw my tongue slowly in broad laps over her clit, making her shiver again.

She doesn't make a sound, she never does, but I can hear the intake of her breath. I can hear the way she holds her breath and then exhales only to take another gulping lungful. She will do this, each time holding it for shorter periods, until she comes. The timing of her breaths is a metronome, letting me know how much closer I am getting.

I slip my free hand down and slide my index finger inside her, into the silken heat of her sex. She is dry, but as my tongue works her clit in slow, wet laps, the moisture of arousal comes until my finger is fairly swimming inside her. I let another finger finds its way into her and press my thumb against the pucker of her asshole. With slow strokes I fuck her with my hand, letting my tongue work itself into a frenzy of quick licks. I can hear her breath coming faster and faster and her grip around my head tightens, her hands painfully caught in my hair.

I don't mind. I'm too caught up in the taste of her, the smell of her, and the sound of her. Let her rip out handfuls now, it wouldn't matter. Her thighs bunch and I turn my fingers into curves inside her. My lips, my chin, are slippery with her and I move my head from side to side, breathing noisily from my nose, and her whole body goes stiff. Her breath whooshes from her and she says my name in an inarticulate gasp. I feel her clenching and unclenching around my fingers and I wait for the waves to subside before I remove them.

Her body goes limp and I withdraw from

her, an almost painful separation, and I rock back on my heels. I am the one looking up at her again and she is gloriously mussed. Her face and neck are flushed, her chest is still heaving, and her eyes are heavy-lidded. She takes a moment to compose herself, then reaches out and slowly wipes my mouth with the palm of her hand. She gives me a curious look. "What was that for?"

I chuckle softly. "Let's say that tonight, I'm your biggest fan."

And I am. I want to applaud her. Was this also an act, a performance for my pleasure or unadulterated realness? I am, as always, left guessing. But sometimes lying to one's self can be so sweet. I simply sit there, smiling at her, and she laughs with something close to childish abandon. Then she reaches down and enfolds me in her arms. She presses her lips against mine, her breasts brushing against my own breasts, and there are so many things promised in that kiss.

When she pulls away I am the one who is flustered. I can feel the quick beat of my heart and the flaming of my ears. She takes my hand, pulling me up. "Let me change and then we can go home." Her smile, the suggestive tone of her voice, and the lure of her ass beneath the flimsy skirt speak volumes. At this precise moment I don't care if it's an act. I'm beyond caring if it's a reality. I just want whatever it is that beautiful body is promising me.

Morning Glory

When the night is almost spent and the edges of the sun peek above the horizon. When the dew is fresh on the grass and I can smell the tang of water on the breeze blowing through my window. After another sleepless night has passed me by and I feel as if I will die . . . the numbness in my body, the tingling of my limbs, and the dull throb-ache in my skull . . . and the edginess of my soul. This dawn, this beginning, this is when I think of you.

Once there was the quiet aloneness of mornings that I savored; a cup of coffee and solitude, a break from life. It felt endless and tranquil. It was a moment, a thread of life captured in sticky amber. It was a globe of time trapped in hardened honey, but I knew you were in the bedroom—dozing away the morning. And I knew you would rise with a smile on your lips and would hold me and tickle me with your half-beard until I laughed or begged for you to slide within my slick walls, whichever happened first. Knowing you were near when I wanted you was enough. Alas, I took that presence for granted.

Time moves on. So does the world. So do we. You are no longer here. I lay here in the morning . . . dawn. I clutch the shirt that smells of you, though the cologne is beginning to fade, leaving me with nothing but the scent of my own sweat. I taste my own salty tears when I kiss the wrinkles, tracing the patterns of the words with a fingertip. It was once your favorite. I bought it for you at the last concert we went to . . . the one where you were enamored of the violinist and I of the conductor.

The mornings are still so quiet. The mornings are still empty. They are still my alone time, but the knowledge of your absence robs it of its poignancy. This knowledge robs me of my solace and my comfort. There no longer seems a point. All the day is empty, so what is there for me to escape from? Morning blends with afternoon; night is the only difference in the sounds and smells. All becomes one.

You are no longer here. You will not rock me to dreamless sleep. You will not comfort me and still the demons that cavort in my psyche. After all, were you next to me, I would not be sleepless. There would be no insomnia. You were the closest thing to God I ever found. When love touched me . . . when I saw love and felt love . . . you became the center of my universe, the lord of my heart, and I knew I had found the divine. I knew I had tasted ambrosia. I knew what life was.

It was the way you touched me . . . worshipped my breasts with the reverence of a gourmand . . . stroked my slick skin with feather-light fingertips and sometimes raked your jagged nails across my back. I remember your soft lips pressed against my knees, my lower back. It was the way you cupped my ass when you fucked me slow, and soft, and sweet, sliding inside me until I could feel it in my tummy, pulling out, the tip teasing my lips—only to do it all over again. Driving me mad with the pace of it until I'm begging, twisting the bed sheets in my hands, for you to come violently inside me.

But you're gone. Dead? No, it might be easier if you were. Then, you would be beyond my reach, gone from me, and there would be nothing I could do. But instead, you left me, left me to my insomnia and my nightmares and my memories, shattered my world with one sentence, one slam of the door. Slipped from my grasp and I am empty, frustrated, alone, and afraid. I am the teenage girl you fell in love with once again.

I lie here in the dawn. There is no beautiful man with the smooth forehead to greet me with bouncy morning wood. There are no bad-breath kisses on my cheek or cold hands on my hips. There's no wiggle of eyebrows or gnarly toes poking at my shin. There is no you. And I lie here, remembering the first time you fucked my ass.

I came so violent when you touched my clit, leaned forward, and slid a finger within as you pumped. I was filled and filled and filled and I thought I would explode. I did. A shower of molten white light in my closed eyes. My whole body shuddering, bucking, convulsing around you and against you. I was numb afterwards, exhausted. I'm still numb now. I cannot forget.

I recall the last time you kissed me—the roughness of your face against my cheek, the taste of mint, and the whiff of the aftershave I bought you for Christmas. It was the quick fleeting thing that plagues a marriage. Ah, had I known, had I but known I would have savored it. I would have savored you, held your head to my breast and traced the rivulets of water down your cheek.

I would have made love to you one last time. I would have shared my morning with you, tried to capture the silence and the stillness and serenity of my mornings in the perfect thrust of your hips, in the effortless slide of your cock within me. We would have been poetry in motion as I pressed my lips to yours and traced the outline with my tongue. A perfect dance. . .

I love—loved, will love—you and the dawn has become so lonely. Come home to me. Rise above the edge of the east, framed in the liquid golden rose of the sun, like a halo around your familiar face. Come home to our bed and come home to the darkness of my sex. Slide through the door, slide between the sheets, slide into me again. Sheath yourself in my flesh, the wet depths of my womb. Let me take you in and feel you and love you. That is home. Come home this dawn and every dawn after. . .

I no longer want such quiet mornings.

Seems Like...

Seems like last year we were teenagers with thick, clumsy fingers, carrying out our will in graceless fumblings beneath my grandmother's apple trees. The blossoms were arrayed around you like sacrifices to the Earth Mother. Your eyes were like the ocean I'd never seen and your freckles were cookie crumbs on your fair skin. I wondered if it was your braces that filled your hair with such static or if it was simply your electric personality.

Seems like a few months ago I watched you come to me dressed like a queen. Your freckles had faded and your smile was broad and metal free. You refused to wear white but were resplendent in cloth of gold. You smelled like apples and peppermint and pear. I heard nothing the priest said; my eyes were filled with you and you and you. When I kissed you I tasted communion grape juice and chalky antacid.

I made love to you underneath the new

moon in a tropical paradise and the darkness gave nothing to me but fleeting impressions. I wanted to see you in your glory, to see the mouth that shaped those pleasurable sounds. I wanted the moon to be swollen like your sex and show me the roundness of your breast and the flush on your neck. I wanted to see, but instead I made love to you in the cloak of night and my senses were a thousand times more acute. The memory still makes every part of me tingle.

Seems like a few weeks ago I carried you across the doorstep of this house that is ours, you with your belly big with our first child. You laughed and danced and twirled even with swollen feet. You glowed with an inner light that made my breath catch in my throat and your eyes were even bluer than the ocean we had finally seen together.

Seems like a few days ago I made love to you again and again in the hammock outside the kitchen window. The breeze slipped past my bare back and stirred your autumn hair until it lifted and moved around me like tongues of flame branding my skin. It is a brand I will carry for a thousand years, even hotter than the trail of your kisses that moved down my spine. Your eyes had become lined and the silver in your hair was like fine wire. I wanted to pluck it and wrap it around and around your finger to form a new ring.

Seems like yesterday you mocked me with a voice raspy from so many cigarettes, but still distinctly your own. I chased you with vigor and pinned you against the wall, smothering you with sloppy kisses until, laughing and crying and begging, I released you. It was only for us to repeat the whole charade once more. In the end we landed in a sweaty, exhausted, laughing heap of flesh on our bedroom floor, and in this private moment, when stillness settled, I could see. I could see the places where your skin was less taut and your breasts less pert, but you still smelled like apples and pears and peppermint.

This time we had together did not seem long enough. It was not long enough. It passed me by with only a blink of my eye, a twitch of my finger. I remember and remember until it all blurs together in some fast-paced montage and I can barely make the details out. There remains love and love. It went by too fast, too quickly. Give me another few years.

Give me another thirty and I will make them last. I will cherish their sweetness like I did the heat of your mouth and draw out each action into an endless moment. I will make each second an eternity, if just to have more time with you. I'll spin it out and roll it thin, just to the point where it tears, to make it longer and seem more full, even though I know it will be nigh unto transparent. But just a little longer and I would willingly fool myself. Time passed too fast and I blinked once too often.

Time is a one-way street and I am only a man. I can turn back the clock, but I wouldn't even be fooling myself. Only now, as I drop the apple blossoms onto your fair body, still so lovely, so beautiful with dim freckles, can I cherish the past. I wish I could see your eyes. I wish I could smell your skin again. I would imagine the trace of apples and pears and peppermint beneath embalming fluid.

I would warm your cold lips with the heat of my body and the flare of my desire for you, and I would let my tears fall in the dark place between your legs. I would make love to you again, hold you again, if I knew that it would break the enchantment. You are my Snow White in her glass coffin and only my sperm can rouse you to life again. I would do these things and more, if only to see you laugh again, feel your hot breath on my neck again, feel your heat around my sex again. I am only dreaming, pretending like the young man you once knew. There will be no tomorrow and there is no longer any time.

Lizzy With Stars

And I taste the bitter alcohol on my tongue, exploding in a frenzy of bubbles against the roof of my mouth. I swallow and gasp for air. Why do I drink? Because it helps the memories pass; because for a moment I am a wild, reckless Amazon creature.

I am the secret inner part of my mind, Lizzy with the stars in her hands.

Forced laughter and I watch him over the rim of my glass. I want this man to want me. I know in the back of my head that he shouldn't matter.

And Lizzy whispers feminist propaganda in my ear.

He does not want me and I walk home alone. Melancholy and pensive, I wonder if I will ever find passionate, confusing, befuddling love in this world. I sing snatches of songs to pass the time and pull my coat closer.

It is cold, but I do not mind. I welcome

it—feeling chapped and windblown with pretty apple cheeks. It is cleansing, this full-scale chill. When I make it to the apartment I begin to cry. These extremes, these self-inflicted tortures, they purge me. They make me whole again.

And Lizzy whispers comforts until I feel numb, apathetic, gone.

I smoke a pack of cigarettes and wander listlessly around the rooms, kicking old shoes and discarded clothes out of my path. The alcohol fuzz begins to fade. I feel worse than before. My head throbbing, my hand strays to the telephone and I dial a set of familiar numbers. Old habits die hard and Lizzy preaches to me. There is no answer, just a machine. I leave no message, but he will know.

And I wait. Moments, hours? Not long. There is a knock and upon opening the door, I find him there. Tall and thin with blue-black hair and green eyes—cat eyes that watch me as, lithely, he moves like liquid silk flowing through my rooms. He sits on my bed. Clothes are removed one item at a time. I see myself through his mind as he watches me from under lowered lashes.

Diminutive only in height; chestnut hair, short, curly, and disheveled, a haphazard crown around a pointed face; wide blue eyes and freckles standing out against pale skin.

Dirty feet and callused hands that make miracles upon his skin—sagging skin, tight and loose in all the wrong places. I imagine he shoves away disgust.

Naked, he sits cross-legged on my bed. I feel his hands move up my thighs, pinch and twist my nipples through the rough fabric of my sweater. My skin crawls. I close my eyes and let the pain wash over me. It is a small thing.

Lizzy stands in my mind's eye, crying to heaven, wading in blood.

He, Dmitri, pulls my hair, tugs my head back, and his teeth are on my neck. I stand there, feeling. To feel . . . not the half-person I have been. The heat rising and quivering electric thrills in my clitoris. Teeth swarming all over me. Thick flesh now red and bruised as he strips me, pushes me onto the bed, strong hands forcing my thighs apart. Cruel fingers prodding and nails raising streaks of red. I need this.

Lizzy cowers and my mind is sobbing, gibbering, but I ache to be closer. Purification and disinfecting, I fade and melt in the red haze of his hands, the vapor of his breath as he bites my lips and twists my arm behind my back. I will die in the flames, crumble to ashes, dust, in the intensity. My vaginal walls contract on nothing and I beg him to hit me. Sharp sting on my buttocks and there are tears. Salty firewater, I am the phoenix, thunderbird. I will rise again. Lazarus. Resurrection. Rebuilt from flames. New, heal me. Punishment and renewal. Oh, and to feel. That is the true thing. The feeling that makes me whole, that mends me.

The covers are rumpled and I see fatigue in his cat eyes. But it cannot stop. Now I am eager, hungry, craving. Let eternity come. I want this all, now. My hands dance soft over his skin and I bury my face in his crotch, feel the hair coarse on my cheek and smell his musky fragrance. I taste salt and the thick texture of pre-cum sliding over my tongue. Swirl around the head, gentle suction.

He grabs my shoulders, pulls my hair again, tearing me away then pressing me down. My breasts quashed against my body. He takes a place behind me—and I feel him plunge, hands in my hair once again. Sweet heat engulfs me. Tears again as he pounds—yes, tears. I will drink them from a golden cup and relish the taste. Open arms, open flower, blossoming. Growing, greedy. I swallow it, begging for more. Fucking me, scrotum bouncing against my clit.

Feeling, breathing, being. Concentrating on the pain. Splashes of yellow dancing in front of my closed eyes and I hear his breath ragged. I am the world eater, the soul ripper. I will consume, take all he gives me. Alive, real, here, now. Mortal.

And it is done. Over too soon as he leans against me then rolls away. I cover my eyes with my hands. My whole body aches. I am tired.

He pulls his clothes on and takes the check from the coffee table, leaves my home. I do not sleep, but luxuriate in the sensations. Sore muscles and raw skin. I feel free, awareness soaring above me.

Lizzy emerges from my euphoria. Sparkling skin and gentle chiding voice. But I am sated . . . no longer empty.

Newborn stars fall from her hands, like diamonds in my eyes.

Ravages of Time

It's raining a fine mist that fills the air, surrounding everything in gauzy strangeness. It might even be my own concrete version of the Garden of Eden if the sky were not so black and the air not so cold. It's ugly weather and it fits my mood. After the fight it fits so well. She said things I hope she doesn't mean. I said things that were true, too true. I said things that I would not normally admit, but anger loosened the steel trap of my mind and it all came rumbling forth in an ugly torrent.

I'm sitting here on this tiny concrete pad that passes for my porch and I'm watching the miserable rain. It drips from the eaves of the house onto the scraggly bushes that are half-choked with dying weeds. Huddling, hunch-shouldered under an old blanket, I feel like a transient or some pathetic stray. I watch the rain. It's preferable to replaying the earlier sequence of events in my head.

I want to forget, even if just for a moment. I want to forget the ugly black hole in the middle of my stomach and the taste of disgust like old pennies and rust in the back of my throat. I just want the monotony of the rain-slicked streets and the sweet taste of cheap jug wine on my lips.

It would be better if I could sleep, but my house smells like her and that's all I can see when I close my eyes; her eyes, swollen and red, smeared with dark clumpy streaks of mascara and filled with hate, anger and all sorts of nameless things I have never seen there before. Her lips were swollen too, puffy and red from our kissing fit. I found them terribly irresistible, like a ripe strawberry. But her lips too were angry, compressed into a thin line.

She looked so much older, so tired, when she was angry. I still wanted to fuck her though. I can smell her sex still on my hands and in the blanket. I could smell her sex still when the fight began, coating my half-mast dick. She had peppermint breath and dark beneath that, menthol cigarettes and coffee, familiar smells and tastes. I can't think of a time when she had ever tasted differently, when her warm breath had ever smelled differently. But she still seemed older.

Once upon a time, in her anger, she

blazed. It was like a fire behind her eyes. She was righteous and indignant. She was a shining star of conviction, like some female messiah. Now she just seemed old. I was watching her, not really listening. I was seeing her as if for the first time.

There were deep lines around her eyes. They weren't crow's feet from all the laughter that I remembered. They were sharp and etched deep, like ravines in her skin. When did she become so hard? Her gold hair, I saw, was waxing silver and the lushness I craved so often was melting away. She was no longer a Rubenesque creature of verdant Earth Mother curves and ripples, but a sharp angular thing. She was becoming a delicate squawking bird.

I couldn't listen to her anymore. Her words meant nothing, nothing to me at the moment. They were just a high-pitched whine in my ears, the buzz of a mosquito, grating on my nerves. I lost all urge to fuck her. The arousal left me, left my dick limp like a deflated tire. I wanted to fuck what she used to be. I wanted to make love to the glorious woman I fell in love with and she was not her anymore. She was just a shadow, a poor facsimile.

Inevitably, I told her to leave. Naked and trembling, she slapped me. I simply handed her clothing to her, ignoring my stinging cheek.

There were many things inside me that I wanted to say, so many tears I wanted to shed. I wanted to mourn for my loss. She was dying. I could see it, smell it beneath the scents of sex and perfume, the smell of age. She was fading away and I wanted to vent my grief, but there was only one person to whom I have ever cried. She was no longer there. She was gone, like a breath of summer in an icy land that disappears beneath the onslaught of cold winds—or the leaf that fades to brittleness in autumn. She was gone and I told her to go away. Away and away and away, far, please. Her presence was salt in my wound.

She wouldn't go. She lashed out, cutting me with her words. The harder I pushed the harder she pulled, dug in her heels. She didn't do it for love. She did it because she wasn't finished spewing her ugliness out of her hard, bitter mouth. It was a torrent, a rush of verbosity. She was hurt, I knew. I could see her shrink, wilt, and sag. For a moment, a brief flash in my mind, she was herself again; the mental picture I carried of her. Arousal came flooding back and I wanted to make love to her on the hardwood floor, bury myself in her embracing warmth. I wanted to lick away the salt of her tears and bask in the warmth of her breasts. I wanted to slide my cock into the tight wetness of her and touch her beauty again.

Yes, this is what I wanted. I wanted to connect with her again. I wanted the point where our bodies met to become the center of the world, the navel of creation. I wanted to taste and know and feel her lips again. I wanted to touch her soul.

It faded to repulsion though when she hit her knees, crying, kissing my shriveled dick. Where was my proud woman and who was the needy thing in her skin? I couldn't . . . not again, no longer. I couldn't even look at her. I dressed her myself, slowly and carefully. Tender, not because I wanted to be, but because I knew no other way to be. I propelled her, weeping, out the door and turned my head when she tried to kiss me. I turned away from her slobbering, questing lips.

In that moment, I spoke, truly spoke from my heart. "Go, please. Just go." Those were the last words I said to her. Those were the last words I felt needed to be said.

She is gone and now I realize there were so many things I *should* have said but didn't. There were so many things I should not have said. It's done and I'm alone with the questions dancing in my head.

Where did the years go, the time go? When did she fade? When did she become paler, thinner, and a ghost? What memories did I have but brief flashes of lovemaking and summer sunlight? What words of hers would linger in my mind? I am hurting. I am confused. I do not understand what happened.

Ah, I am a liar. I do. I know what happened. *Time* happened, and I have no control over that. I can only watch it slip through my fingers like grains of sand in an hourglass and regret, regret, regret so many things.

I'm sitting here, miserable in the rain. I cannot put her from my mind and all I really want right now is to drink this wine. It won't heal me. It won't heal the hole in my heart, but it will for a time, mend the memories I have of her. It will sculpt her, new and blazing in my head. I will see her, newborn, with newborn eyes. I will forget that she is slowly dying. I will forget that I can see death creeping up, that I can feel her mortality hovering above her. I can recall what she was and banish the scarecrow thing she has become. It won't heal me, but it will help for a time.

Fate

Sunlight streams through the window, falling warm and golden on his skin. The air is heavy with the scent of vanilla. My body feels heavy; bloated and sotted with sex—indolent with it, a contentment filling me. Fingertip to fingertip, he smiles into my eyes, dazzling my heart.

"Soul-mate," he says.

"You believe in soul-mates?"

Palm to palm. Love line, life line. "Of course. Don't you?" There is mirth in his voice.

Silence is my answer. Answer enough, as we draw closer. Hip against hip, breathing each other's breath. Tangle of white limbs. We melt together; one pulse, one destination.

* * *

Asked by a friend, once, how we met, we share that look that lover's share; share that laugh that lover's share.

"Coincidence," said I. "Kismet."

"Ka," he concurred, ever the Stephen King fan.

Later that night I whispered to him of a "she" that I yearned for, a woman to share the beauty of our simple joys, a woman to make of us a Trinity; a Holy of Holies for the altar of love. Together we would blaze with the white light of righteousness. What is more noble, more sanctified than love?

He stroked my hair as I dreamed out loud. "Ka-tet," he said before we drifted into sleep.

I looked it up the next morning. *Ka-tet: a group tied together by destiny.* As I read, I tasted the word, pleased with the sound of it in my ears and the feel of it on my tongue. Speaking it, I gave voice to my hope and later I would say a prayer of thanksgiving to Mr. King for such a useful term.

* * *

Snow is falling, lacework melting on my cheeks and caught in his lashes. It's fresh enough to cover the gray city in eerie luminescence under the pregnant moon. Half-drunk we ham it up, teetering from sidewalk to street. I sing "Greensleeves". He serenades me with "Henry VIII". A cat screeches, someone in an apartment curses. Headlights flash into my vision.

I see beauty in his eyes, promises in his smile, before I stagger back, screaming. Crunch of gravel and bone. The music of shattering glass provides a tempo to my sobs. Strong arms and strong coffee banish my tears but not the sight and smell of blood or the memory of the driver's drunken, blubbering apologies.

The world has shattered, like a snow globe dropped and forgotten. Melted snow on my gloves. The priest speaks of God's will and I ask him about karma. He mutters at me and waddles away. A doctor approaches me. I swear I can see the white planes of his skull beneath the grim expression on his face and I turn away. Clutching a blonde nurse's hands, looking into those green eyes for a hint of spring, I ask her desperately, on the edge of panic, about crystal balls, tea leaves, and prognostication.

She hands me four Xanax and a telephone number.

* * *

A snow globe of glitter and lace sits on the night stand. Three wise men, the magi, watch us through their window. Déjà Vu. Legs intertwined. Fingertip to fingertip.

"Am I your soul-mate?"

I smile, press my palm to hers. "Very much so."

Her blonde hair against my dark. "As much as him?"

"As much and as equal." Pain in my heart, still. Is it in my voice?

Fall into her. Blazing and burning. Bathe in her waters. Melding. She fills my lungs. I breathe with the tide of her blood and shelter in the dark of her womb.

* * *

I watch her sleep, grateful for her presence, filled with the knowledge of her. But I am divided, aching. My soul is split and I can't mend it.

Kismet, ka, predetermination, destiny, whatever word you might choose to call it, it is the same. It is the unavoidable, the inexorable, the insidious, the unyielding. Without it he would still be alive: kinetic and dynamic. Without it she would not be here, warming my sorrow, touching my tears. Ka-tet. I found mine, but already shattered. Too soon or too late. The stars had it in for me. It is my lot.

Cruelty.

Mar

The sea has always had a hold on me. I was born in the water, in the heyday of homeopathic at-home births with incense burning and drums tapping a counter beat to my mother's grunts. I swam before I walked, I'm told, and even tried synchronized swimming once on a whim. "Waterdancer", my parents called me, but today I am just myself.

It wasn't any surprise that I bought a home on the Gulf, within walking distance of the dirty water and the tides that called my name. I called my little bungalow, "Caballito del Mar". I saw those words on a billboard once. They made me laugh. "Little horse of the sea", little seahorse. I thought of sea monkeys playing water polo on beds of well manicured seaweed with coral castles in the background and mermaids with hair of purple and blue rippling in the currents as they watched over vast herds of grazing animals. The stuff of childhood fancies, this Caballito del Mar, but the first time I sat on the porch of my new home, I knew the name was right.

On that hot day, dirty bare feet propped on the rail, taste of beer making me crave more and the sound of water in my ears, I saw them; rolling, prancing, stamping, snorting, living in the surf. Water horses. Caballitos del Mar. They sang with the voices of whales and danced with the grace of dolphins. Their eyes burned like ice lit with dawn and they tossed their heads, proud and cruel. I painted the words in blue wavy lines above my door.

In my dreams, she comes from the sea with eyes as gray as leaden swells and hair as wild as kelp. She rides the caballitos up to my doorstep. Sand covers her cheek and she drips saltwater onto my tiles. She tells me her name is Maria. Maria tastes like fresh oysters and I swear there are gills behind her ears.

These days I don't swim much. I can feel the ebb and flow in my blood. No matter where I go, I feel the tug, the draw of the sea, in my marrow. We are naught but saltwater to begin with. Sometimes, all we need is a reminder and the thought stays with us. I could no more distance myself from the sea than a fish could, but there is no reason to swim. I feel buoyant and floating as I walk.

And I walk a great deal. On the mornings after the dream I wake up with salt crusted lids, sand in my sheets and a wobbly, sick feeling in my gut; craving tuna, oysters, salmon, shrimp . . . something to settle my stomach. And then I walk, traversing the dusty, little-traveled roads that wind through the hills behind my home. I ignore the heat and welcome the sweat. For lunch I like to stop at the fruit stands and eat melons and grapes as I watch trucks packed with migrant workers zip past.

The dark-eyed women with their black braids and dark-eyed children (of the earth, so earthy) who take my money and offer me the choicest fruits whisper behind their hands when they think I am not listening. *"Bruja. Sangre de mar, de agua. Mira los ojos de ella. Muerta caminando."* Witch. The sea in her blood, water in her blood. Look at her eyes. Walking dead. I cannot disagree with them.

She is like Venus, borne upon a seashell to the shore, pulled by the caballitos. I greet her with a smile and with an ache in my heart. Her hand is cold and slick in mine and I'm afraid I will damage the webbing between her fingers. She laughs at my concern and kisses my hand before pressing it against the horses. They are cold rushing water and primal anger. They are Poseidon's earth-shakers and Gaia's sacrificial well. She urges me to ride, but some deepness in me protests. We make love on the sand and she laughs, the shells in her hair tinkling like chimes.

I see them every day now. Manes of curling spray, beards of kelp, and hoofs of coral. They are calling to me. I watch them from my porch. My body aches for Maria and my tongue longs for the taste of her skin, the liquid coolness of her on my parched throat, the burble of her voice in my ear. The caballitos toss their heads, jerking an invisible thread, inching me closer. As if they are saying, "Come, come, we shall take you there." Castles beneath the sea. I am afraid, so I walk.

My parents come to visit and my mother wonders when I will find a man and have children. My father asks me about the fishing and the rental price of a jet ski. My elderly grandmother peers at me, sniffs me, and speaks to me in a strange Irish-Southern brogue that only my cousins and I could ever understand. "Yew smellin' of the sea with no salt in yer hair. And yer eyes are fire, yer hands are scales. Has yew seen the maighdean-mhara? Her and the

Auighsky comin for yew." She peers at me with a gimlet eye and my blood is colder than water.

Tonight I swim, beneath the moonlight. I know I am not dreaming, but I feel as if I am. The water is thicker than blood, thicker than thought. Thick like a dream, as I pull myself through it, bubbles trickling from my mouth like a trail of bread crumbs. She rides the caballito, hair streaming behind her as if in a wind, keeping pace with me.

Maria laughs, a high pitched echoing sound that pounds at my ear drums and she speaks, her words are distorted but clear enough. "Ride the waves with me. Fleet as wind, speeding through the spray, you and I. Naiads together. I'll show you the depths where there are creatures that glow and we can make love in my bower of coral. Come and meet my father whose beard is the kelp and his rage are the storms. The sea is in your blood."

I want to believe her. Instead I surface, breathing and gasping. A snatch of a song comes to me. "It's true you ride the finest horse I've ever seen. Standing sixteen one or two with eyes wild and green. I could never go with you, no matter how I wanted too." Tears, salty tears, wash down my cheeks, indistinguishable from the water, save for the trail of heat they leave on my face.

She bobs near me and bares her teeth. "You don't believe that." She reaches out and touches her nails to my face. "Waterdancer. Come with me, come home. Answer the call of your blood."

Blood. Blood warm. The waters of the Gulf are warm as blood. Mother's womb. Back to the beginning. We all begin with saltwater, with saline. Her words make so much sense. And her eyes lull me with their calmness, their agelessness. She has seen the tides of a thousand years fall on the shores of a thousand nations.

She melds her body to mine and wraps her arms around me. She is warm as the water, skin soft. Her hair winds around us like living tendrils. "Come. Come with me. I have chosen you among all the others. You can see the horses."

And I can see them, impatient as they break the surface, and I remember their anger and their fury. But Maria is close. Inexorably she draws me towards the caballitos.

They are solid between my legs—a surging column of water that sends shocks and shivers through my spine. Maria is behind me. We plunge towards the blackness, away from the moon. The creature is unbound and unrestrained.

I would be frightened were it not for the pebbled hardness of her nipples on my back and the feel of her sharp teeth on my ear.

Down and down. My lungs will burst. Fire in my brain. She tells me to breathe. I can't. I want to live. So badly do I want to live. She holds my arms tight with a strength I would not have guessed from her. "Breathe," she urges me again and again. I do not want to die. She squeezes me so tight I think my head will explode. "Breathe!"

So I breathe.

Has anyone ever spoken about the sensation of drowning? I cannot do it justice. It is the sudden cold rush of the liquid. You are breathing, but there is nothing *to* breathe. Exhale and try again. You are a fish out of water. You have given up.

The darkness overtakes me.

I wake upon a slab of marble. Tiny polyp jellies move in front of my eyes and I hear the songs of whales. With wonder, I breathe, and my hair ripples behind me as I explore my webbed fingers and my clawed toes. With eyes as gray as surface swells she watches me, smiling a sharp smile. "You had only to believe," she says to me and then points past a circular opening to where the caballitos graze.

<u>Other books by Logical-Lust</u>

Swing!
Adventures in Swinging by Today's Top Erotica Writers
Edited by Jolie du Pré

SWING! is a stunning anthology of swinging adventure stories from some of the world's top erotica writers, compiled and edited by Jolie Du Pré.

Being edited by Jolie Du Pré, you can expect some hot, sizzling sex stories, both well written and highly creative. We don't pull any punches when we say we expect **SWING!** to be one of *the* top erotica releases of 2009!

ABOUT THE EDITOR

Jolie Du Pré is an author of erotica and erotic romance. Her stories have appeared on numerous Web sites, in e-books and in print. Jolie is also the editor of **Iridescence: Sensuous Shades of Lesbian Erotica**, published by Alyson Books, and is the founder of GLBT Promo, a promotional group for GLBT erotica and erotic romance.

<u>SWING!</u> **is published in multiple digital (ebook) formats. Get your copy direct from <u>www.logical-lust.com</u>, or from Amazon (Kindle) and other worldwide online retailers!**

Messalina – Devourer of Men
by Zetta Brown

When life imitates art. . .

Eva Cavell is a woman with an embarrassing secret.
She is sexually frustrated and is convinced that her size and race intimidates men.

In an attempt to relieve her sexual tension, every Thursday Eva goes to a local movie theater and allows desperate strangers to fondle her in the dark. She allows no eye contact, no phone numbers—and definitely no names.

During one of her escapades, renowned artist, Jared Delaney, a smooth Southern gentleman with irresistible violet eyes, has Eva breaking her own rules. He has been watching Eva on her weekly visits and sees through her icy defence and straight through to the hot passion burning underneath.

. . .expect to be framed

Messing about in dark theaters isn't a good pastime for Eva. She is a tenure-track instructor at a private Denver college that is currently embroiled in a sex scandal and she is the youngest child of a prominent black family.

To add to her turmoil, Neil Hollister, Eva's classroom aide and former student, is a handsome, barely-legal frat brat whose interest in her is carnal rather than academic—and she's tempted.

Despite desperate attempts to maintain control, Eva's world is spiralling into chaos. As emotional pressures build inside her, an explosion is imminent. Will she ever be able to live her life how she wants and without shame? The answer may lie with a woman who is bold and unashamed in her sexuality.

Can Eva be more like her? What would happen if she even tried?

<u>Messalina – Devourer of Men</u> is available worldwide in paperback and digital (ebook) formats, direct from <u>www.logical-lust.com</u>, or from Amazon, Barnes & Noble, and all good retailers!

Crimson Succubus: The Demon Chronicles
by Carmine

"A few years back, I began receiving emailed submissions to the erotic literary ezine *Sauce*Box* from a writer known to me only as "Carmine". These submissions were short pieces ('flash-fiction', if you will) detailing yet another *"Tale of the Crimson Succubus"*. Each was a stand-alone jewel, horrible, cruel, fantastically, outrageously, graphically sexual, but also somehow (dare I say it . . . forgive me, Carmine) charming. I liked them very much and published every one that was sent.

"Now I find that some these short tales along with longer pieces concerning the 'adventures' of the Crimson Succubus, and a third section concerning a mythical nymph Mytoessa who also becomes involved with the succubus have been collected together in one place—a delightfully, tastefully disgusting book, **Tales of the Crimson Succubus, The Demon Chronicles** by Carmine.

"This person, Carmine, is one sick puppy, but one with adorable eyes and floppy ears. The tales involve much blood- and semen-letting, murder, torture, deception and pain, but at the same time, I often want to laugh and wish that the creatures would appear for real, in front of me, so that I could see with my own eyes and even touch (very, very carefully, mind you) these monsters formed from the primordial slime of all of our great cultural myths.

"And of course, like all myths, these tales speak to our deepest fears, and hopes and fantasies . . . perhaps to archetypes from times before even the written word, times long forgotten in consciousness but remembered in the collective genetic code. I don't know. Whatever. They're a great read, an exciting read and one that will tickle your nightmares and daydreams long after you've put this book down."

Guillermo Bosch, Editor: *Sauce*Box*, Ezine of Literary Erotica
Author of **Rain** and **The Passion of Muhammad Shakir**

Crimson Succubus: The Demon Chronicles is available worldwide in paperback and digital (ebook) formats, direct from www.logical-lust.com, or from Amazon, Barnes & Noble, and all good retailers!

Future Perfect
A Collection of Fantastic Erotica

By Helen E. H. Madden

What if you made love to a woman at the end of the universe, only to discover she was devastating black hole? What if the archangel Gabriel fell in love with the Virgin Mary and never delivered the Annunciation? What if a female dominant saw the future . . . every time she had an orgasm? For years, speculative fiction has asked the question "What if. . .?" Now the tales of *Future Perfect* go one step beyond and speculate on the possibilities of the erotic.

From the distant future to a biblical past and everything in between, *Future Perfect* examines the role of sex in a fantastic world. The stories range from hard science fiction to urban fantasy, but through it all runs a thread of explicit sexuality that embraces a wide range of orientations and relationships. Whether presented as the force of cosmic creation or the deceitful lure of Satan, *Future Perfect* takes sex beyond the limits of the everyday to show it as the impetus for change on a universal scale.

So open the cover and leave the mundane behind. A world of "What if. . ." is waiting for you.

Future Perfect – A Collection of Fantastic Erotica is available worldwide in paperback and digital (ebook) formats, direct from www.logical-lust.com, or from Amazon, Barnes & Noble, and all good retailers!

Lightning Source UK Ltd.
Milton Keynes UK
30 August 2009

143215UK00001B/13/P